# TEMPTATIONS OF FATE

## VEIL OF SHADOWS

### BOOK TWELVE

## M. R. PRITCHARD

# About Temptations of Fate

### M. R. Pritchard

Lucifer's return looms, his voice calling from beyond the grave, driving Alastor to the brink of madness. With the realms teetering on the edge of chaos, Meg finds herself held captive by the one person she never imagined. As the veil between worlds weakens, darkness threatens to consume everything—and time is running out to stop it.

# ONE

*THEN*

SPARROW WAS A FALLEN Angel turned Hellion turned walking dead turned Raven King. It wasn't all for nothing. He'd cleared his family curse by sacrifice. He'd done as instructed by the remaining Archangels. If he wanted his family land, he had to purify his blood. And hers. So he did it the only way he could; he killed her. He stabbed her in the heart with a blade that made her bleed out every drop of his blood she'd ever consumed; it erupted from her body and killed her for twenty-four minutes. Their bond was severed.

# TWO

*Now*

SPARROW HELD MEG'S WRISTS; no more of her blood would be spilled. Not in his Kingdom. Nowhere else if he had a say in it. Meg's expression was one of horror and shock, as though she couldn't fathom a worse person to stop her from ending it all. Her body had turned to stone beneath his grip. Wide blue eyes stared up at him. Disheveled dark hair stuck to her lips and she was breathing erratically.

Sparrow released her wrists and stepped back, his hands up in surrender to show her he was safe. He wasn't sure she'd ever believe it, but the thing he'd done, he'd done for her–for *them*.

Meg moved faster than he'd expected in her weakened state. She grabbed another piece of the broken mirror and held the sharp fragment to his neck.

"What the fuck?" she finally spit words like hate. "Where am I?"

Sparrow stepped back until his spine and wings hit the wall. She looked equally as though she might devour him with rage and collapse on the floor from exhaustion. It was the dead blood Alastor had fed her. Clearly it hadn't dissipated from her system even though she'd been sleeping for weeks.

"You're safe," was all Sparrow said.

"If you are here, I am not safe," Meg sneered. She'd cut her hand with the shard of glass she was holding to his neck and blood dripped down her thin wrist. "Let me go," she demanded.

"Can't do that." Sparrow took a side step toward the bathroom door. "I think you should lie down."

"Let me go," Meg demanded with rage in her eyes.

"Go lay down, Meg, before you fall flat on the floor."

Blood dripped. Sparrow stilled and did not lick his lips. Instead, he scowled at her, annoyed that she didn't move, irritated that she wouldn't listen to him.

"I will kill you," she threatened.

"Why would you want to do such a thing?" Sparrow took another step to the side.

Meg took a step forward. "Because you deserve it. Because of what you *did*." She stumbled and fell into the doorframe, her broken wing scraping the wall, and she hissed in pain. "Because you *hurt* me." A broken heart was more than hurt. He'd scarred her to the core.

Sparrow didn't move to help her. Understood if he moved a muscle in her direction, she'd stab the shard of glass into his body. "You should go back to bed."

"You should shut the fuck up." Meg reached over her shoulder and pressed a hand to the broken bone that was sticking out of her wing. It would never heal with how badly it was damaged. She glanced toward the bedroom door. "Let me out of here."

"No." Sparrow took another step backward.

Meg's stomach growled, and it echoed throughout the room.

Sparrow glanced down.

"Don't look at me," Meg seethed.

"Lay down," he ordered.

"Fuck off," she snapped. She took a breath, collecting her energy, then pushed off the door frame and took a step toward the Raven King, murder in her eyes. "I want out. Now."

"Nope." Sparrow shook his head.

"I..." The hate in Meg's gaze vanished as her eyes rolled to the back of her head and she collapsed.

Sparrow waited, ensuring she didn't wake, burst to her feet, and stab him in the neck. She wanted to. That was easy to see. He toed her shoulder with his boot. She didn't wake, moved little more than shallow breaths. Sparrow crouched and peeled her fingers away from the shard of mirror. He took it to the sink and collected the rest of the broken glass, wrapped it in a towel, and set it outside the door to the room. He glanced at the bed, then to her limp body on the floor. She'd hate him for touching her, but he was going to do it anyway.

Sparrow stooped next to Meg and rolled her, protecting her broken wing. He slid an arm under her shoulders and another under her knees, then lifted. She was too light–

nothing but bones, her cheeks gaunt. He wasn't so sure about Teari's recommendation of Tincture of Time for the dead blood to clear her system. Sparrow set Meg on the bed and looked her over. He got a cloth from the bathroom and cleaned the blood off her hand and wrist. He watched her thready breaths. A hand went to his pocket and fingers slid over the vial of blood. He'd been waiting for the right time to give it to her. He couldn't wait much longer for her to recover. Alastor was wreaking havoc on Hell and the Earthen plane. They needed to put a stop to it, but they needed Meg well.

Sparrow took the vial out of his pocket, flipped off the cap and dripped the blood into Meg's mouth. Then he turned tail and made fast work of getting out of her room. If she woke with fresh blood in her system, she'd probably have the strength to rip every feather off his wings. But Sparrow didn't feed her fresh blood. It was bagged like the Hellions would drink. Just enough to sustain her. He closed the door and locked it.

Picking up the towel filled with broken mirror, he made his way out of the bunker. He waited at the main door, listening closely to ensure no one was wandering the forest who might see him. Gabriel had taught Sparrow plenty, more than his own father. Always have a place to hide your people during disaster. When Angels had inhabited the Earthen plane thousands of years ago, they'd built shelter in the mountains to stay hidden and survive. The same kind of shelter worked well for Gabriel during the Fast-Zombie War, his kingdom surviving most of the massacre, when the other Archangels weren't so lucky. They didn't have a place to hide, thinking that the Seven Kingdoms of Heaven were completely safe. No realm was safe. And Sparrow was glad he'd heeded Gabriel's advice during the rebuild and had constructed the bunker in the small ridge of mountain at the edge of his Kingdom.

Not hearing a thing, Sparrow opened the door and exited the bunker. He made his way to the main house and made a mental note to remove everything sharp from Meg's room. The flash of her teeth crossed his mind. He couldn't remove those, unfortunately.

The Legion were in the training yard, the rest of his staff busy with daytime duties. The walk to the main house was uneventful. Sparrow was glad he didn't run into anyone. He surveyed the path in the distance, hoping not to see the dark flash of Nightingale's hair as she hounded him. He couldn't really explain the towel he carried, filled with bloody shards of mirror. He made quick work of returning home and disposing of the mess.

# THREE

THE SUN WAS SETTING AS JED DROVE THROUGH the sleepy town of Perdido Key. The sky was painted in hues of pink and orange across the horizon, a stark contrast to the darkness they had left behind.

Tires crunched over a seashell driveway as Jed pulled up to the small beach house. It was dark and quiet. He'd had driven all day and night; over fifteen hours through the Carolinas and Alabama, states none of them had ever been to and didn't have time to peruse. Each time they used a rest stop, Jed drew more runes on the Jeep Grand Cherokee that they were driving. He'd darkened the windows and carved a shrouding spell into the roof. He could never be too safe after the disaster at the Peabody Library.

Shay reached for the door.

"Wait," Jed warned. "Let me check it out."

Shay sighed. "I'm sure it's fine."

"Listen to him," Chel grumbled from the cargo area where he was sitting. The Hellion barely fit. Shoulders hunched and wings awkwardly tucked away, Jeeps weren't designed for the comfort of a Hellion. "Believe me, if anyone wants out right now, it's me," he muttered.

Jed surveyed the beach house on Parasol Place. There were rocking chairs on the front porch and the yard was fenced. There was privacy and the soft sound of the ocean nearby was relaxing. He went to the front door, held his hand over the lock, and whispered a spell. The door opened. Jed flicked on the lights and searched the house. He found nothing surprising. The beach house was small and simply decorated. It seemed too quaint for Meg's tastes and the lack of books would have them all going stir crazy. They'd have to find a library or bookstore. Satisfied with his findings, he made his way back to the Jeep.

Shay was watching him as he walked closer.

Jed decided he liked the way his boots crunched on the crushed seashells and the smell of the ocean air. He opened Shay's door and helped her out. "All clear." He smiled.

They all piled out, the sea breeze instantly wrapping around them. Shay took a deep breath, savoring the salty air. It was a new beginning, a much needed respite from the chaos they had fled.

"Whoa," Jed stopped Chel. "We gotta do something about those wings."

"Who cares?" Chel looked around. "No one is here." He sniffed the air then his face twisted in confusion. There was no one for miles. He glanced at the nearby houses and apartments, not smelling any inhabitants.

Jed whispered a spell that hid Chel's wings from sight. "Come on, let's check out the beach," Jed said, a rare smile spreading across his face.

Rue and Remington ran ahead, their laughter echoing

in the evening air. Chel followed, his eyes scanning their surroundings.

The light from sunset was so bright it hid their auras.

Shay and Jed walked hand in hand, the soft sand beneath their feet. The waves lapped gently at the shore, a soothing rhythm that calmed their weary souls.

Rue and Remington were splashing in the shallow water. Remington cupped his hands and shoveled ocean water at his sister as she shrieked in delight.

"This place is beautiful," Shay whispered, leaning into Jed.

"It is," he agreed, pulling her closer. "Their auras aren't like up north. The sun is brighter here."

"Hopefully the moon too." Shay kicked off her shoes and dug her toes into the soft sand. She'd never lived in a place that didn't require closed toed shoes or boots year-round. She had a sudden urge to buy flip-flops.

They stayed at the beach until the sky turned dark, the stars appearing one by one. And the moon *was* bright enough to hide the children's light.

Reluctantly, Shay called Rue and Remington out of the water and they made their way back to the house. Everyone was exhausted from the white-knuckled escape from Peabody Library. They had been afraid of being attacked while they drove.

They made their way back to the house, their earlier excitement giving way to yawns and drooping eyes.

Inside, Shay was glad to find a room for the children and a master suite.

"I'll take the couch," Chel said, bending to look out the windows.

Jed and Chel secured the house, making sure all was safe. They marked the doors and windows with runes of charcoal and salt.

Shay helped the children get settled.

"I'm hungry," Rue said.

"Well," Shay said as she searched the cabinets. "There's not much here." She found bags of expired chips and cans of expired soups. "This stuff might still be edible." She piled the items on the counter and found plates and bowls. "We'll have to go to the store in the morning."

Remington was standing in front of the pantry. "There's a lot of soda here."

Silence fell on the group. Shay glanced to Jed.

"Has our mother been here?" Remington asked.

"A long time ago," Shay said.

Remington turned with cans of orange soda in his hands. He gave one to Rue with a look, then passed the rest out.

"I'm sure she's okay," Chel said. "She has to be okay."

Cans popped open and Shay held hers up. "To bright sunshine."

"To sunshine," Jed echoed, a sense of hope filling the room.

For the first time in two days, they felt a sliver of peace. The road ahead was uncertain, but for now they had each other and a place to rest their heads. And that was enough.

"Where is Nero going to sleep?" Rue asked.

Jed nearly spit soda mid-swallow. "If I see that horse again..."

"Hey," Shay argued. "Be nice. There was a reason for what he did."

"To get us all killed." Jed slammed his can down. "There was no good reason for what he did."

"Don't judge him so harshly," Shay said. "We don't know."

Chel grumbled something about stupid animals.

———

THE MORNING BROUGHT heat and sun. Jed messed with the air conditioner, using more magic than handyman skill to get it working correctly.

"I want to go to the beach," Rue said. "It was so pretty last night. We've never been to the ocean before."

"Someone needs to go to the store," Shay said as she made a cup of coffee. Meg had an entire cabinet stocked with coffee. It was strange since she barely drank it in Hell.

"I can go," Jed offered. "You all can go to the beach."

The kids found shorts and T-shirts, Jed promised to look for swim suits while he was at the store.

"We are wholly unprepared for a beach," Shay said digging through her suitcase to find something. She settled on an old T-shirt and faded jeans and decided to sacrifice them to the cuts of scissors. "We need flip-flops, sunscreen, sunglasses, and hats."

Jed glanced at Chel. "I'm not sure they'll have your size in anything."

Chel looked up from his cup of black coffee and grumbled. "I'm not a beachy type of guy."

"You can't be going there in Hellion gear and combat boots." Shay was searching a hallway cabinet for towels. She found a stack, walked toward the front door, and motioned to the children. "Let's see if this daylight is enough."

Everyone filtered outside, shielding their eyes.

"It's a miracle," Jed said, staring at the children. "Not a speck of aura."

It was true. The Florida sunshine was so bright there was no aura visible. What little they'd seen last night was completely bleached out by the sun's rays.

# FOUR

Alastor was covered in dirt, and as he dunked his head in the bathtub to silence the demands of Lucifer, the tiny finger bone slipped out of his shirt pocket and floated in the dirty water. Alastor snatched it up as though it were gold. He set it on the nearby table as the door to the ballroom creaked open.

An overpowering presence entered the ballroom and Alastor instantly recognized it.

"What do you want, Raven King?" Alastor wiped water from his face.

Heavy footsteps echoed as Sparrow made his way across the ballroom to the nook where Alastor was holed up.

"You could have chosen one of the smaller rooms," Sparrow frowned, taking in the disarray.

"That would seem too permanent." Alastor tore off his shirt, dried himself, then dug through a suitcase to find fresh clothing.

Sparrow rocked back on his heels. "Have you considered a deal with Babylon for the fallen Queen?"

"I will consider nothing until she brings me to Lucifer's bones." Alastor plucked the finger bone from where he'd set it, tucking it in his pocket again. He made his way to the leather club chair and sat. "There was a horse here. A Demon horse. Shay's horse. Why was Shay's horse spying on me?"

Sparrow's brow rose. "The Crossroads Demon is a creature of Hell. I would know nothing about that."

Alastor smirked. "I think you know more than you let on."

"You took the throne. You should be aware of your realm." Sparrow took a step closer to get a better view of the map.

Alastor's mood shifted as he rubbed his face. "I want to be done with this." He knocked his knuckles against the side of his head. "I'm tired of Lucifer's voice in my mind, driving me insane."

"You know who is good at finding bones of family members? Meg, she found Clea's." Sparrow noted the new portals.

"You want her?"

"I've told you. Babylon does." The poor bastard couldn't remember much these days.

Alastor waved his hand to the sky. "Go find her."

Sparrow cocked his head, questioning. "She's not here?"

"Hellions scared her away. Said she disappeared." Alastor scoffed. "She can't be disappearing anymore since her Ouroboros has been cut off. The creature is stupider than a box of baboons." He turned to the window. "She's out there somewhere. Running."

"So you're ready to trade her?" Sparrow asked.

"With the agreement that she delivers the bones the next time I see her face."

"She may need some convincing."

"Do whatever you need. Take her soul. I'll increase your soul share ten percent." He exhaled a heavy breath. "I want to be done with this."

"Something new on your mind?" Sparrow asked.

"A Demon called Asmodeus is vying for the skin trades. I need to shut him down. Lucifer was nothing to me before this. I want him out of my mind, out of my life." Alastor suddenly screamed out in pain and fell to his knees, holding his head.

He didn't stop screaming. The sound echoed in the giant ballroom, making Sparrow's ears throb.

Sparrow stomped across the room and grabbed Alastor by the back of his shirt. He dragged the Demon to the bathtub and threw him in. He pressed a hand to Alastor's neck and shoved his head under as deep as he could.

Alastor's eyes flashed open with terror before slowly calming. Sparrow pitied the Demon; seemed the only time the guy had peace was when he was a few heartbeats away from death.

Sparrow held him under the water. The thought that he could end this Demon right now and take the throne of Hell crossed his mind. Wouldn't that be something special? Holding a throne in the Seven Kingdoms of Heaven and the throne of Hell. There were no Deacons to say anything about it. There was no balance. Only power waiting to be taken. The sensation of a thousand rocks dropping in Sparrow's gut startled the thought away. He gripped Alastor's shirt in his fist and pulled the Demon out.

Alastor leaned over the side of the tub, water sloshing onto the floor as he sucked in giant lungfuls of air. "Thank you."

"I'll find her," Sparrow promised.

———

Sparrow left the slowly breaking Demon in the ballroom and made his way to the winding stairwell. He climbed up the stairs, two at a time, and took a right. He walked down the hall until he found Meg's room. He kicked the door open and was greeted by a familiar scene. Sparrow knew Meg was always a bit of a mess, but she still lived life one heartbeat away from running for her life. She'd always been like that. Sparrow went to her closet and found the bugout bag near the door. He glanced at her clothing, grabbed a pair of boots, and then searched the room for her blade. He tucked everything under his arm and left, doing his best to focus on the door and not the bed.

He found her blade in the Hellion lair amongst the rotting bodies of her Hellions. Sparrow wrinkled his nose. Alastor was not doing the throne of Hell any justice by letting the castle deteriorate. He paused, recognizing the decomposing body of Skeele. No feelings passed through Sparrow. The Hellion was Sparrow's second in command when Sparrow was a Hellion Commander, and then Meg's lover, the father of her bastard child.

Sparrow left the lair and made his way to the closest portal, eager to leave the disarray that was now Hell.

# FIVE

Gabriel paced the dimly lit chamber, his wings tucked tightly against his back. The room, a secluded corner in the heart of Gabriel's hidden catacombs, was filled with the flickering light of oil lamps casting long shadows on the walls. The last Deacon lay on a bed, his leg heavily bandaged. The air was thick with tension and the scent of medicinal herbs. Teari kneeled at the bedside, changing the gauze wrapping around the Deacon's leg.

"Alastor has officially taken the throne in Hell," Gabriel said, breaking the silence. His voice was a mixture of frustration and concern. "Things are bound to escalate."

The Deacon winced as Teari tightened the bandages on his severed stump. He took a deep breath, trying to steady himself before responding. "Alastor's rise to power was inevitable. But with Meg... she's more vulnerable than ever. We need to find her before he does."

Teari glanced up, her hands gentle but firm as she finished securing the bandages. "Meg is strong, she thinks she can face Alastor alone." Teari was shaking her head, hating that Meg had pushed everyone away. Nightingale had told her what happened. She hid her children, banished Noah and Nightingale and Thrush, and took on Alastor and his army of the dead with just her Hellions.

Gabriel rubbed his chin. "The balance of power in Hell is shifting and it's not in our favor."

"What about Babylon?" Teari asked.

Gabriel was silent for a moment too long. It didn't convey that Babylon was completely ignorant to the situation in Hell as he'd previously indicated.

Teari finished her work and stood, wiping her hands on a cloth. "Meg is missing." She reminded them.

Gabriel made a face.

"What?" Teari demanded.

"She's not really missing any longer." Gabriel looked away.

Teari was on her feet and in front of Gabriel in a heartbeat. "Excuse me?"

"She's safe," Gabriel said.

Teari hated that she was outside the loop of information.

The Deacon nodded, wincing as he adjusted himself on the bed. "Time is of the essence. Alastor can't wait. He'll be hunting for her, just as we are." The Deacon took a heavy breath. "I need her to find the feather of truth. I need it. We all need it to maintain some balance in this world."

"Where is it?" Gabriel asked. The last time he'd seen the relic was at Meg's trial, nearly fifteen years ago.

"It's at the Safe House in Auburn." The Deacon leaned back in bed with a heavy groan.

Teari crossed her arms to reassure herself. "We'll find

her. And when we do, we'll make sure she understands the gravity of the situation." Teari knew Meg had secrets that needed to stay that way.

"Every moment we delay is a moment Alastor gains the upper hand," the Deacon said.

With that, the room fell into a focused silence as they began making their preparations, each aware of the immense challenge that lay ahead. The fate of Meg and the balance of power in Hell depended on her.

# Six

"What do you have under your wing?" Nightingale asked Sparrow.

"Mind your business, sister."

# SEVEN

*MEG*

I FEEL HUNGOVER. Like, the worst hangover I've ever had in my entire life. I drag myself out of bed only to fall on the floor.

There's a tray of food and a glass of blood. Fresh blood. It smells decadent; better than chocolate, better than anything. The feeling of retching crawls up my throat, memories of the last time I had blood following it. Alastor had given me and Chel blood from the dead... I don't trust it. I don't know where it's from. I pick up the glass, take it to the bathroom, pour it down the toilet, and flush. My mouth waters. I hate myself for doing it.

There's no mirror in the bathroom. I lean against the doorframe and remember. Sparrow was here. Fucking Sparrow. I'm going to kill him. I glance back at the toilet. I should have drunk the blood. I cross the room to the tray and pick up a bottle of ginger ale. Gross. Inspecting the bottle, I notice it's sealed and not expired. Looks fine. I crack it open and take in the sweet hiss of carbonation. I drink it. No, I guzzle it like I've crossed the desert with no water. Ginger ale is far from my favorite but right now it tastes better than anything I've ever drank in my life. There's a bag of chips and a sandwich on the tray. It's been a long time since I've eaten real food. My mouth waters as I pick up the sandwich and sniff it. Turkey and cheese. Smells wonderful. I consider that it could be poisoned, but I'm starving and not queasy for the first time in ages. Food poisoning is easier to overcome than rotten-blood poisoning, or at least that's what I tell myself. I bite, devour the sandwich, and wash it down with the ginger ale. Then I break into the bag of chips and pour them into my mouth like an animal. As I'm chewing, something dark slouching against the wall catches my eye. I move closer and recognize my bugout bag. Wait... how did that get here?

I pick it up and go to the bathroom, checking the contents. I lock the door and turn on the shower and get clean. As I wash myself, I touch the scar on my upper thigh where my birthmark used to be. At least it's healed.

Wrapping myself in a towel, I take out a change of clothes, thankful for the T-shirt and jeans. After getting dressed in my own clothing and not the black sweats, I feel slightly normal.

I drape my bag over my shoulder and walk toward the bedroom door. My hand hovers over the knob. I could be anywhere. I glance down at my feet, wishing I had shoes. To my surprise, the doorknob turns when I twist it and the door opens.

There's a pair of boots in the hall. My boots. This is all

very suspicious. I don't see anyone else. I don't smell anyone. As I'm stepping into my boots, I glance down the hall. It looks like I'm in some kind of underground bunker. It's massive with a dozen or more doors down one end and a large opening to the other end.

Why would Sparrow leave the door unlocked? Why would he give me food and my bag? Why would he leave the door open? He's up to something. I'm still going to kill him as soon as I lay eyes on him.

My footsteps echo as I walk down the hall that opens into a great room. Not far away, I see a giant door that could only lead outside. As I'm making my way toward it, the metallic sound of locks opening echoes. I still and look around. There's nowhere to hide. There's only couches and end tables and a dining area.

The door opens and a dark figure steps inside. "See you're upright."

There's a lamp to my right. I pick it up and throw it at him.

Sparrow steps to the side and the lamp shatters against the wall, missing him.

"That was uncalled for." Sparrow says, a deep frown creasing his face.

"It was *very* called for." I search for something else to throw at him. If I had the strength I'd pick up a couch and whip it at his head.

"Are you going to beat me up and run off? You will not get far with that broken wing." He looks me up and down. "And you didn't drink the blood. Do you care about living? What if it wasn't me who opened that door?"

"I don't care."

"You need to care if you gave a fuck about surviving."

I scoff and take a step away from him. "My only plan is to kill you. I'll deal with surviving later."

Sparrow chuckles. "Save your energy."

"For what?"

"Babylon. The council wants to speak with you."

My mouth snaps shut. I wasn't expecting that. I'm in Heaven. Shit.

He kicks the broken lamp to the side and reaches for the door to the outside. "Follow me and keep quiet."

Sparrow holds the door open as I pass. We are standing in a dense forest. I turn and see jagged rocks of a mountain that go up and up and up. A soft metallic noise clicks and something sounds like fabric falling. I focus where Sparrow is standing and notice the door is now hidden.

"Keep up." Sparrow walks through the forest. There's no path and in the fading light I can barely keep up.

I stumble, my broken wing hitting a tree trunk, and I hiss in pain. It's quite brave of him, turning his back to me after everything we've been through.

He steps to the side as though he can hear my thoughts, then he picks up his pace. In the dusk, he doesn't look like much more than a moving shadow. We finally make it to a path.

I follow behind him, imagining all the ways I can kill him from this position. I wish I had my blade. It would be easy to stab him. He's so tall though, and I can't fly with this broken wing. I'd have to touch him—climb up his back and slit his neck. Or I could scrape his spine with a dagger at the base of his backbone. He walks like a God. Those big stupid black wings drag on the ground. Memories of featherless wings flash behind my eyes. An empty church. Glue. Feathers of every color. Sparrow's mouth on my body. My breath catches.

His head jerks to the side and I get a good look at his profile. Yes. He's just as handsome as he's always been. Moreso with the confidence he now carries. And that lingering darkness is about as tempting as a line of cocaine at a disco party.

Self-hate floods my body. I shouldn't be looking at him, not after Skeele sacrificed what was left of his short life to me. I look away, stare at anything but him. I do my best to find attractiveness in a stick on the ground. I pick up the stick and snap it between my fingers. Unfortunately, it doesn't compare to the Raven King and the thought of snapping his pretty neck.

Someone is on the path ahead. Sparrow steps to the side, blocking me from view. I keep my mouth shut like he asked—not because I want to follow his demands, but because I don't feel like fighting anyone. Whoever it is makes their way down another path, away from us.

The sky darkens and tiny lights illuminate the path. I notice a house in the distance but Sparrow leads me away from it. I recognize the house and the side lawn where we fought. I shiver and shake my head, chasing away the memories. I don't want to think of that now. I can't think about how the one man who broke my heart into pieces and nearly killed me is standing so close to me right now.

Instead, my thoughts turn to Skeele. My steps slow as pain aches in my chest.

"It's just a little bit further to Babylon," Sparrow says.

"Thanks for making me walk there," I mutter.

Sparrow makes a noise of exasperation. "If you think I'm getting in a vehicle with you, you're nuts."

"I'm nuts?"

"Yeah." He chuckles. "Way nuts."

"You're nuts." I jab a finger in his direction.

He shrugs. "Been worse."

We reach a stone wall with a gate. Beyond is Babylon.

Sparrow unlocks the gate and swings it open, motioning for me to pass.

I creep through and still. The canopy and forest that once camouflaged us is gone. The streets of Babylon are wide open. The walkway to the center looks like a park with perfectly manicured shrubs flowers. The path is lit with streetlamps and the splashing water of the fountain echoes.

"Walk faster," Sparrow says. "Or the Angels will start staring."

"How would they even know who I am?" I ask.

"Everyone knows the fallen Queen of Hell."

Ouch.

We make it to the courthouse where the Archangels hold their secret meetings about the world and lay down judgement and look down their perfect noses at everyone.

Sparrow opens the door and holds it for me. What a gentleman. His boot stomps down in front of me and I stumble to a stop.

"I swear to God if you try anything I'll stitch your lips shut. Do. Not. Bite. Anyone." Sparrow glares at me.

"Fine." It's not a promise but I'll try my best because I'd rather get the heck out of this place and get back to my children. I must tell them that their father is dead. They need to know Skeele died by my side, a hero; that's what

I'll say. I'll spare them the gory details. They don't need the mental image of him being consumed by Alastor's chaos.

———

ALL THE ARCHANGELS ARE HERE: Michael, Raphael, Uriel, Raguel, Saraqael, and my father, Gabriel.

Sparrow moves away from me and takes his father's seat. That seat is empty because I killed Sparrow's father. Remiel was a bastard anyway, no great loss. He never did his time as a Hellion and as a result, Sparrow and Nightingale suffered. I have no remorse for putting an end to that Archangel.

I glance at Raphael and lick my lips, remembering how he screeched like a chicken and fainted when I bit him. Loser.

Gabriel stands. "Meg, it's wonderful to see that you are well."

"Am I though?" I ask.

"I pray." My father's blue gaze narrows on me, compelling me to mind myself.

"Thank you." I glance around the table. They're all staring.

"This is a bargain for your freedom." Gabriel sits and motions to the chair next to me. I sit, leaning forward so my broken wing doesn't catch on the back of the seat.

"Why should anyone be bargaining for my freedom?" I ask.

"You are a prisoner," Michael says.

"No I'm not," I say.

"You are," Sparrow says, his gaze narrowing on me. "You are my prisoner."

"I am?" I ask. He looks too dark amongst these assholes, the only one with black wings and dressed like he's black-ops. The rest are white-winged and dressed in flowing robes like a church choir. The contrast is astounding.

An awkward silence passes through the room. Gabriel clears his throat. "Without the Deacons, Babylon will maintain the balance between realms."

A laugh bubbles up out of me.

Gabriel glares and I go silent.

"What do I have to do with that?" I ask.

"You need to fetch the feather of truth from Hell and deliver it to us," Michael says.

"Then you'll have your freedom," Raphael adds.

"You want me to go back to Hell?" I ask.

"The feather of truth resides in the Auburn Safe House," Raguel says, his tone snide.

If I had a choice in who to kill next, I'd pick Raguel.

"Alastor is trying to resurrect Lucifer," I tell them.

"We are aware," Gabriel says.

I glance to Sparrow.

His gaze is empty.

"Do I get a choice?" I ask.

"Not really," Raphael says.

"Perfect." I stand.

"We'll escort you to the fountain so you don't get sidetracked by anything," Raguel says.

———

BEING ESCORTED by six Archangels and Sparrow is a daunting moment in my life. I was the Queen of Hell. I shouldn't be intimidated, but here I am with no throne, no Hellions, no family, a broken wing, and a dry throat–amongst other things. I feel like I'm walking the plank.

I stand at the edge of the Fountain of Eternity. My heart beats against my ribcage.

"It will take you to the Nightjar's pond," Gabriel says.

I nod. I've gone through this portal before; came through it to free Gabriel after the other Archangels turned on him.

"Don't jump without saying goodbye," Sparrow's voice is behind me.

I want to tell him to fuck off, but I can't find the courage.

"Take this." His hand touches mine and opens my fingers, he presses cool metal into my grip. I look down and recognize my blade.

I gasp and turn toward him, eye to eye since I'm standing on the edge of the fountain.

"One day," Sparrow says. "If you're not back in one day, I'll come for you."

I don't know what to say. But I don't have time to say anything because he shoves me into the fountain before I can stab him with my blade.

# EIGHT

Sparrow stepped back as the fountain took Meg to Hell. Unease flooded his chest. Sending her like this was not right. He wished she'd drank the blood before leaving. She would have been stronger. He felt the weakness in her back as he'd shoved her into the fountain.

A heavy hand landed on Sparrow's shoulder. It was Gabriel. The other Archangels had wandered away to their own kingdoms after Meg disappeared beneath the water.

"You think she can do it?" Gabriel asked.

"She must," Sparrow replied without looking at Gabriel. It was hard to say much to the Archangel he'd disappointed. Gabriel wasn't his father but he was once Sparrow's superior. Sparrow was Gabriel's Legion Commander for a time, before he was banished for losing Meg and before he did his time as a Hellion to break the family curse. But Sparrow had moved on to bigger things, like nearly killing Gabriel's *special* daughter. Not one of the hundreds of other children he'd helped give life to. Gabriel must've understood there was a deeper reason for all that had transpired, because Gabriel threatened Sparrow's life once and then they never spoke of it again. Probably because Gabriel now knew the full story and he'd tried to intervene in their relationship before with disastrous results. The Archangel had received an omen just like the rest of them. And he'd tried to intercept fate.

Gabriel squeezed Sparrow's shoulder before moving away. They walked together for a few feet before Gabriel said, "How long are you giving her?"

"One day," Sparrow replied.

Gabriel nodded in agreement. "You let her go with that broken wing." His tone was concerned.

"She'd rather kill me than let it get fixed."

"Could see that," Gabriel said.

The dimly lit walkway was heavy with tension. Gabriel's presence cast a faint glow in the shadows. Sparrow gazed into the darkness, his expression stoic but his eyes betraying deep concern.

Gabriel faced Sparrow, his wings flexing. "Sending Meg back to Hell to find the feather of truth is reckless," he said, his voice tinged with worry. "The risks to her are unimaginable, especially if Lucifer is resurrected while she's there."

Sparrow pressed his eyes closed. "I know the dangers. We don't have a choice. Without the Scale, the balance of the realms is in jeopardy. The council will never give Meg a moment's peace. They will always be on her hide. You know this."

Gabriel's brow furrowed. "Hell is more dangerous than ever with Alastor on the throne. She might not survive. This could be the dire ending to Clea's omen."

Sparrow sucked in a breath, trying to steady his

emotions. "You think I haven't thought of that? You think the worst outcomes haven't come to my mind?"

Gabriel's eyes softened. "You care for her deeply."

Sparrow spat out a horrified chuckle. "Don't let her know. She thinks I hate her. What can I expect after what I did?"

"It's been a long time. So what is your plan?" Gabriel asked.

"Alastor thinks I'm in Hell searching for her. If she's not back in one day, I'll find her." This was a dangerous game Sparrow was playing. One that could have dire consequences if Alastor figured out Sparrow was in on this for more than just souls and power.

Gabriel sighed, the weight of the situation pressing down on him. "If anything happens to her…"

Sparrow nodded, his blood had turned to ice with thoughts of her injured more, or dead. "I know."

"Keep your kingdom under shadow," Gabriel warned before veering toward his land.

Sparrow's lungs begged for air, he couldn't take a deep enough breath. At least she was safe in the bunker and he had control of the situation. Now he had control over nothing. He'd given her one day, but one day was too long. He didn't trust Alastor or the Hellions he employed. Hell was no longer Meg's safe space.

Sparrow launched himself into the sky and flew the rest of the way home.

He'd spent twenty-four years without her. Then nearly another fifteen. What was another twenty four hours? She might despise every fiber of his being, but he'd make sure she knew the truth when she came back. He'd sit her down and explain everything in a place with no weapons and... maybe he'd put tape over her mouth.

Without his grace, Sparrow was something different. And Meg had helped transform him when the Scarecrow convinced her to stab him in the heart.

# NINE

Jed rose from the bed. Shay was sound asleep and didn't stir as he made his way out of the room. He moved quietly through the darkened beach house, careful not to wake anyone. The soft sounds of the ocean waves outside the window echoed throughout the house, a soothing backdrop. He reached the door, turning the knob slowly to avoid any creaking.

Just as he was about to slip outside, a voice cut through the darkness.

"Where do you think you're going?" Chel sprung from the couch.

Jed turned to find Chel standing in the middle of the living room, his silhouette barely visible in the dim light. Chel's eyes were sharp with suspicion.

"I have to speak with someone," Jed said, hoping his nonchalant tone would be convincing.

Chel crossed his arms. "At this hour? You're up to something. What is it?"

Jed met his gaze, determination in his eyes. "I need to talk to the Crossroads Demon."

Chel paused, tipping his head to the side as he realized what Jed was saying. "Just speak with Shay here."

"No." Jed was shaking his head. "I have to make a deal with them. With her."

Chel studied him for a moment, then sighed. "Alright. But if you're going to do this, you're not doing it alone. I'm coming with you."

"You can't," Jed said. "You need to stay here with the kids."

"I don't like this," Chel warned, glancing toward the closed door of the room where the children slept.

"You don't have to." Jed stepped out into the cool night air, the sound of the ocean growing louder as he moved away from the house. He didn't have to go far to find a crossroads; he walked down the street to find a paved inter-section near the beach parking lot. He didn't want to be seen, but he doubted at this hour many would be awake. All the lights were off in the surrounding buildings. In the time that they'd been at the beach house, Jed hadn't seen another soul. There were people in town, at the stores and driving down Perdido Key Drive, but in the surrounding block and beach, no one. It seemed Chel was right when he mentioned the homes were empty surrounding the beach house.

Something tore in Jed's chest. He didn't want to put Shay in this predicament but something was coming, some-thing dark and dangerous. This town was eerily quiet, barely populated and seemed to be stuck in a different era. Maybe that was the south since the Fast-Zombie War.

Maybe people could feel the thinning of the Veil and that was the only explanation for what he'd seen while shopping. The empty beaches concerned him. He didn't trust Meg, knew that this was her hideaway all those years ago when she went missing for weeks and they'd sent Skeele after her. She'd done something to this town and he was surprised she'd kept it a secret this long.

He took a piece of chalk from his pocket and summoned the Crossroads Demon.

———

NERO WHINNIED with delight when he saw Shay at the crossroads.

"Where have you been, boy?" Shay threw her arms around his neck and squeezed.

Nero neighed a response then went still as stone when he noticed who'd called them.

Shay turned slowly and faced Jed. Her eyes went wide. "You? No." She shook her head. "Jed, you can't do this. You can't make a deal with us." She settled a hand on Nero's neck. "I won't let you."

"I need to make a deal." Jed's hands flexed and he stepped closer to the rune circle.

"No." Shay couldn't control her shocked expression or the glare of betrayal.

"You haven't even listened to what I want." His voice lowered. "Please don't look at me like that."

"It doesn't matter," Shay said. "I don't want to make a deal with you."

"You've made deals with hundreds. Why leave me out

of the fun?" Jed asked, a smirk dragging his lips aside. "Something is coming, Shay. And I don't want us to be without protection."

"You've protected us for this long." Shay tangled her fingers in Nero's mane and fought the emotions bubbling in her chest. She didn't want to lose Jed to a Crossroads Demon deal. Couldn't. Jed was all she had in this world. If she lost him, she'd be alone. "You don't want this," she warned. "We are strong together."

"We need to get home, so I'm going to make this quick," Jed said, tucking his hands in his pockets.

"Please..." Shay whispered. "Don't make me do this."

"I want to make a deal for power." Jed tipped his chin down.

"What kind of power?" Shay whispered, afraid of his response. Everyone wanted power or death, she just didn't think Jed would be the one to request it after all he'd been through, after all they'd been through together.

"Enhance my magic for whatever darkness is coming." Jed raised his hands and sparks crackled. "That's it. I don't want anyone dead, I don't want any souls. Nothing other than strength."

Shay bit her lip and met Nero's gaze. Silent communication passed between the two. It wasn't a difficult deal, they didn't have to kill anyone, but to enhance Jed's supernatural power, they'd have to do something unusual.

"Okay," Shay said. "You realize that we will call upon you."

Jed nodded. "I look forward to the day. I will always be by your side," he promised.

Shay's eyes flashed red. The tether that connected her

to Nero went taut. The words that came out of her mouth were not of her own volition. They were compelled by the curse of the Crossroads Demon and Nero. "Out of the eater will come something to eat. And out of the strong will come something sweet." Shay smirked and held out a dusky hand with long necrotic fingernails and a transparent golden ring on her middle finger.

Jed shook her hand and the deal was done.

A shiver passed up Jed's spine. "Already?" he asked.

"Not yet," Shay said. "We must collect something first."

Jed rubbed his foot over the chalk line and tugged Shay into his arms. He kissed her, hard and desperate. "I wouldn't have made the deal if I thought we didn't need it." He searched her eyes for anger or hurt. He'd hurt her too much in the past and he never wanted to see that disappointment in her eyes again.

Nero made a noise behind them and Jed turned Shay to his side. "You!" Jed pointed at Nero. "Have some explaining to do."

"He didn't mean it," Shay said. "He was trying to find Meg."

"Did he find her?" Jed asked.

"Yes. He found her." Shay pointed to the marks on his back. "He was injured." Shay waited for more information to come through the tether that bound her to Nero. "Alastor and the fast dead attacked him. The Nightjar healed him. He brought Meg to the Auburn Safe House and left her there."

Jed rubbed a hand down the side of his face. "Shit. Where has he been?"

"At Peabody Library with the Angel." Shay smiled, glad to hear that Nero was some place safe.

"Warn him that there's not a lot of space where we are holed up," Jed said. "A horse on the beach will raise suspicion."

An ache lingered in Shay's chest. She didn't want Nero to be away from her. She moved away from Jed to stroke and hug Nero. "Will you stay?" Shay asked Nero. "There isn't enough room in the house but there's a backyard with a privacy fence."

Nero whinnied in agreement.

# TEN

Nero lay on the warm but comfortable straw bed in the Nightjar's cabin. The clapboard house was dry and empty and the wounds on his backside were nearly healed. The scratches had progressed to dry scabs. The moon glow of Hellsky filtered through the small windows, casting an eerie light across the room. He shifted, turning his attention to the Nightjar's pond. Its surface shimmered darkly. The pond was a portal, but Nero had seen nothing come or go from it since he'd been taken in.

Nero knew the Nightjar was a haunting force, but she'd cared for him. Something tugged at Nero's heart. Perhaps that was all she ever wanted was someone to love, someone to love her. She'd never experienced that. Her unbaptized soul was doomed to wander the night sky because the Archangel Raphael discarded her in Hell. Nero nibbled at the clumps of sweet grass she'd collected. It was night and the Nightjar was out wandering the forests of Hell. He wasn't sure what she was looking for, but every night she left, every night she searched and mourned and moaned.

The Nightjar eventually returned, moving silently around the cabin. Her presence was both comforting and unsettling. She paused by the window, her gaze distant.

"Hell is changing, my baby. And it's not for the better. Not like with the Queen."

Nero's ears flicked forward, a soft snort escaping him.

"Alastor," she replied, her voice barely above a whisper. "He's grown more powerful, more ruthless. He's been digging around the castle grounds, looking for something. The new Hellions follow him blindly, causing chaos and destruction. Something is not right here," Demore sang mournfully. "Something is very very wrong with our home." She looked out the window, in the direction of the burning caves. "The dark days of chaos have returned."

Nero's eyes narrowed at the mention of Alastor's reign.

The Nightjar shook her head. "I don't know what he's searching for. But whatever it is, it can't be good. You must be careful. Alastor is more dangerous than ever. He's searching for you."

———

NERO WAITED for the Nightjar to fall asleep. She curled into a shadow, her form folding in on itself in the corner and disappearing with the sunlight. In sleep she was nothing, at dark she came to life like a nightmare. Or perhaps she went to haunt the Astral realm.

Nero stood and limped out of the cabin, his hooves crunching on the fallen leaves. He didn't want to leave the Nightjar without a goodbye of some kind. He made his way to the road then ran. He'd been running each day since the claw marks on his back started healing, stretching his muscles and gaining back speed he'd lost from the injury. The fast-dead seemed to be gone now. The only dead Nero saw were the slow, lumbering kind—the ones he could easily escape if need be.

He wandered the nearby forest, straightening his aching back and muscles. A noise broke his focus; he perked his ears and heard the sound of water dripping and sticks snapping as someone stumbled. He turned to the pond and saw a familiar form.

A sense of fear and joy flooded him. What was *she* doing here?

# Eleven

*MEG*

I EXIT the portal and swim to the surface of the Nightjar's pond. I make my way to the shore, quietly, taking in my surroundings and wishing I wasn't soaked. I crawl out of the pond, water dripping from my clothing.

There's no sound, just evening crickets. I shrink back after stepping on a crisp twig. The snap echoes. Something feels strange here now. It's no longer my home, no longer my Hell. The brimstone that lingers in the air is more pungent than usual, no longer a familiar scent.

The weight of wet feathers makes my busted wing ache but I don't let the pain slow me down. I scramble up the shoreline and check the sky. There's nothing visible from the clearing over the Nightjar's pond. My eyes adjust to the dark forest. I have over a hundred miles to cover to get to the Auburn Safe House. I need a car or something fast.

A whisper of a whinny draws my attention. There's a black horse walking toward me.

"Nero?" I ask. "Is that you?"

A snort of steam answers as he trots closer and sniffs me.

"What are you doing here?" I ask. "You should be with Shay." I take off my shirt and wring it out, then put it back on. My jeans will have to dry on their own.

Nero turns, showing me the claw marks on his backside.

"Something got to you..." I gently touch the skin near the marks. "It looks like you're nearly healed."

I think of my hundred mile trek. My feet will be covered in blisters with these wet boots.

"Are you feeling well enough to give me a ride?" I ask.

Nero huffs and nods his head. "I need to get to the Auburn Safe House as fast as possible."

Nero tips his head and scrapes his hoof. I think that he's telling me to climb on his back, but he's pretty tall and I've never ridden a horse before. I look for something to stand on and find a fallen tree.

"I've never done this before," I warn him as I motion to the fallen tree I'm about to use as a step.

Nero moves closer.

Getting on his back seems impossible. The horse is huge and the fallen tree doesn't give me much rise. I try to jump and throw a leg over his back but I just wind up kicking him in the ass. He doesn't appreciate it and snaps his teeth at me.

"I'm sorry. I fucking suck at this."

I swear Nero rolls his eyes as he lowers himself to the

ground and shakes his chin, motioning for me to get on. I straddle his back and hold on tight as Nero moves to his feet. He shakes his head, and I take it as a sign for me to hold on to his mane. I tangle my fingers in his coarse hair and hold on as he starts trotting.

Nero makes his way through the forest. The ochre moon in Hellsky casts long, flickering shadows that seem to dance and twist, mocking our every move.

I swear I feel eyes on me, the ever-present gaze of Alastor's Demons and dark creatures. A shiver runs up my spine as Nero makes it out of the forest to the crumbling roadway.

Hell didn't feel like this before, not even in the summers. The night air is oppressive, the heat and humidity making it hard to breath. Sweat trickles down my back. I should have drunk the blood.

Nero starts with a gallop. He whinnies and it sounds like a warning, so I lean down and wrap the strands of his mane around my hands.

"If you can get there before sunup, that would be great," I say.

Nero takes off, faster than anything I've ever experience. Wind blows in my ears. I pinch my thighs together and press my face to the back of his neck. Holy Hell, this Demon horse is faster than...

Before I finish the thought, he stops.

Auburn Safe House is directly in front of me. And my clothing and boots are dry.

I slide off Nero, feeling like I'm drunk or stoned or both. It takes me a minute to steady myself.

"Thanks." I pat his side. "You don't have to stay." I hold my stomach, ready to puke from the fast ride.

Nero whinnies a goodbye before trotting away to do whatever Demon horses do.

I walk toward the half crumbled Safe House. It's familiar, even in its dilapidated state. My boots crunch over crumbled concrete and the front gate squeals as I push it to the side.

As I walk inside, my old mantra surfaces, *never go back to the scene of the crime*. A bad feeling tickles my gut. I pause and grab a flashlight from my bag, the morning light not enough to see clearly yet. Every so often I hear a noise, a distant cry, wails that crate a haunting soundtrack to this task. I push the sounds to the back of my mind, concentrating on my goal: find the feather of truth.

Chairs and tables litter the open room. I recognize the visitation room, the doors that lead to quarantine and questioning. I step over a lonely shoe speckled with blood. Moaning echoes from the corner. I squint and see one of the walking dead headed my way. Damn. I grip my blade, thankful that Sparrow gave it back to me. I shouldn't kill the dead, but without the Safe Houses, they have nowhere to go. It feels wrong releasing their soul only for it to be stuck here, giving Alastor more power.

The dead man moves closer, moaning and shuffling. I take two steps forward and slice his head off. The body drops to the ground. I go still and let my eyes focus on the shadows to make sure there's no more dead.

I recognize the long hallway that leads to where the Deacons held my trial. I start making my way there, sure to be quiet as a mouse. I tuck my hair behind my ears and listen. There's more moaning down the opposite end of the hall. My damaged wing catches on a broken chair and I hiss in pain before crouching to pull the feathers out of the cracked wood. I need to get this fixed. I tuck the feathers in my pocket, not wanting to leave behind any evidence that I was here.

---

I FIND the door where the Deacons held my trial. As I approach the door, I glance around one last time, making sure I haven't been followed. Satisfied that I'm alone, I push open the door and slip inside.

The room is dimly lit. I collapse against the wall, finally allowing myself a moment to breathe. I made it. I close my eyes and rest for a moment, my stomach still uneasy from Nero's speed.

A small scratching sound echoes. My eyes flash open. It could be a mouse or a dead person hiding under the debris. Or maybe those little burrowing owls moved in. I focus on the desk-of-questioning, the three chairs where the Deacons who judged me sat.

I close my eyes and remember... *the feather of truth is white with brown stripes. It's brought into the room on an embellished glass platter along with a gold scale.*

The scratching noise stops and the silence of the abandoned courtroom is unnerving. Dust motes dance in the dim, flickering light from a single broken window high up on the wall. I creep through the shadows, my footsteps echoing slightly on the cracked marble floor.

The once grand room now lay in ruins, the dark wood

of the desk-of-questioning warped and splintered. The jury box stands empty, its seats covered in a thick layer of dust. I move cautiously, my eyes scanning every inch of the room for any sign of the feather of truth. This is like looking for a needle in a haystack. Who knows if I'll find a single feather in here, who knows if it will be the correct one? I glance at my wing over my shoulder. I could just give them one of my feathers. Would they even know the difference? How could Babylon do anything without the Deacons?

"Come on, Meg," I mutter to myself, my voice barely above a whisper. "Focus."

My heart is pounding in my chest as I approach the bench, my hands shaking. The knowledge of what this place once represented, the power it once held, the secrets it will now keep. I once hated this place, now I mourn its loss. The feather of truth saved me, it was the one thing that tipped the scales in my favor when I'd royally fucked everything up. A harsh, hushed laugh escapes my throat.

I search behind the desk, my fingers trailing over the rough, uneven surface. Nothing. Frustration nags at me; I can't lose focus. Where would I be if I were a golden scale and magical feather?

I move to the jury box, lifting the seats one by one, looking for any hidden compartments or clue.

A noise echoes through the empty room, making me freeze. My heart skips a beat as I listen intently. Is it my imagination, or is someone else here? I hold my breath, straining to hear anything out of the ordinary. After a few tense moments, the silence returns, heavier than before.

I continue my search, moving to the witness stand. I run my fingers along the edge, feeling for irregularities.

There is a small indentation, barely noticeable. I press it and a panel slides open, revealing a hidden compartment. My breath catches in my throat as I reach inside.

My fingers brush against something soft and delicate. Carefully, I pull it out. The feather of truth. Its pristine white and crisp brown stripes are a stark contrast to the decay and ruin around me. Relief washes over me but is quickly replaced by a sense of urgency. I have what I need, now I need to get the heck out of dodge.

Clutching the feather tightly, I turn to leave, but a shadow moves in the corner. I spin, my heart racing. The courtroom seems to close in around me, the darkness suffocating.

"Time to go," I whisper to myself, steeling my nerves.

I tuck the feather of truth into my pocket, doing my best not to damage it. I make my way back through the courtroom, my senses on high alert. I can't shake the feeling that I'm being watched.

# TWELVE

NERO WANDERED AWAY FROM THE AUBURN SAFE House. He was unsure of his next move, but he knew he couldn't stay in Hell. It didn't feel right. His flank shivered as the eerie feeling of being watched slid up his spine. It was time to move on. He'd been with the Nightjar long enough and he missed Shay. He was glad to have some answers on Meg and find her alive.

A flash of pink caught his eye, something half buried in the debris on the side of the road. Nero moved closer and nudged it, pushing the leaves and sticks away. A child's doll lay in the dirt. He knew what to do with this. He grabbed the toy between his teeth and made one last stop before returning to Shay.

Nero trotted back to the Nightjar's cabin and nudged the door open. He set the doll near her shadowed, sleeping form then lay in the straw and waited for a formal goodbye.

As night spilled through the windows, the Nightjar's form unfurled and came to life. She stretched her shadows, reaching out in tendrils to explore the cabin. She suddenly turned and focused on Nero as though she were spinning in dance.

"My baby, how are you feeling tonight?"

Nero nodded his head at the creature and neighed softly.

The Nightjar moved around the cabin, brushing away cobwebs and peering out the windows.

"Something has changed," she said. "Something feels off. Can you sense it?" she turned to Nero.

Yes, Nero could feel it. And he needed to leave, promptly. He couldn't afford another injury.

Nero stood and nudged the doll with his nose.

"What is that?" the Nightjar moved closer. "Oh!" her intake of breath sounded like howling wind. "A baby!"

The Nightjar reached down and picked up the doll with her long fingers. She held it to her chest before spinning in a circle. "A baby." She nuzzled the toy. "Finally. My own baby." She stroked its face, and delicately touched its nose, lips, and ears.

She turned quick as a whip to face Nero. "This is all I have ever wanted." Her voice sounded like a distant song, humming from the mountains. "Finally." She hugged it close. "Thank you."

Nero whinnied and nodded before glancing at the door.

"You must go?" The Nightjar's voice was distant. "I don't want you to go but you must." She was nodding in agreement. "Yes, you must. It's changing too fast, I fear. And I must keep my baby safe." She moved to the window, the doll nestled in the crook of her arm. "Alastor will search for those loyal to the Queen. He is twisted and sick." She opened the door. "You must go before he calls you back to the castle and injures you further. Hurry, the fast dead are coming."

Nero tilted his head and recognized the echo of fast moving feet.

He whinnied a thanks to the Nightjar before exiting her cabin.

"Be safe, my baby," the Nightjar called. "My friend."

Nero glanced back and found her rocking the baby doll in folded arms. A memory of Shay rocking him the same way when he was all long legs and injured body flashed through his mind.

Nero nodded one last time before taking off. His hooves broke sticks and crunched piles of leaves as he made his way to the road and took off fast as lightning.

Nero ran until he saw the silvery break in the Veil between Hell and the Earthen plane. He picked up speed and jumped through.

The Peabody Library was different. Nero wasn't sure exactly what was different about it. Just, something. He wandered the edges of the lot, then around the building, unable to enter because of the wards. Someone was inside, he could tell. Nero made his way to the front door and tapped with his hoof.

The door cracked open and a man Nero had never seen before appeared.

"What are you?" the man asked as his face twisted in confusion. "You're not a real horse."

Nero whinnied before nudging the door open and stepping inside.

"Whoa, buddy." The man stepped back and Nero finally noticed that he was an Angel.

Nero reared up on his hind legs and neighed loudly.

"Quiet. Quiet!" the Angel said, shoving the door closed.

Nero galloped through the library, searching. He checked the rooms and the kitchen, then paused when he saw the destruction in the back corridor. He turned to face the Angel, wishing he could speak.

"Alright, you know this place." The Angel kept his distance, eager to avoid impalement by horse hoof. Or worse. "I know you. I saw you break the wards and run off."

Nero advanced on the Angel, neighing over and over again, nodding his head frantically. He was trying his best to express concern for his missing friends and threaten the Angel who didn't belong here.

"They're fine, big boy. They're alive just not here," the Angel finally said, holding his hands up in surrender. "They had to leave." The Angel's eyes searched Nero's. "I've heard about you. The Crossroads Demon horse." The Angel looked in awe. "The first of its kind."

Nero's steps echoed in the empty library as he roamed, moving away from the Angel. He huffed in disappointment. At least Jed and Shay and the children were okay. His back ached and Nero moved closer to the fireplace. He whinnied at the Angel, a demand to explain his presence in the library.

The Angel sat opposite Nero and crossed his legs. "An explanation, okay. I was drawn to this place by two beacons of light erupting into the sky. Being on the Earthen plane, I knew whatever it was didn't belong, but neither did I. There was a large collection of Demon-kind beyond the wards." The Angel was motioning with his hands, making circles and strange gestures, acting out his story. "I didn't want to get involved but then I saw you break through the wards and run away. Then I heard a little girl screaming." The Angel shook his head. "There was a lot of screaming and shouting and that half-Angel man who was here was drawing on a crap-ton of magic. I mean... ha... his aura was *lit* up brighter than the sun."

Nero showed his teeth, urging to the Angel to stay on track.

"Okay. Sorry I got sidetracked, it was just all very impressive. So, I entered the property and fixed the wards outside to stop the onslaught of Demons."

Nero nodded in approval. At least the Angel helped and wasn't the usual piece of shit he'd come to know.

"I met the blue-haired girl." The Angel shook his finger at Nero. "She's like you. Dark and powerful."

Nero nickered an affirmative.

"And there was a Hellion." The Angel chuckled and held his stomach. "I was not expecting that. A mish mash of creatures all being kept here in this library. The strangest were the children." He tapped his chin. "There's something about those two. I just can't place it. The boy looked slightly familiar." The Angel paused before shaking his head as though he were shaking away a bad dream. "Anyway. They packed their bags and left. Headed south. They said I could stay here and protect the place. Which was perfect because I needed a safe place to hide." He held arms open. "It was kind of a miracle, after all. I'm on the run myself."

The Angel exhaled loudly, pressed his lips into a straight line and raised his eyebrows in an awkward expression. He shrugged. "That's it. That's my story."

Nero stared before whinnying in approval. Then he set his chin on the floor and gazed at the fire.

"Are you hungry? I have some fresh carrots from the farmer's market. They're organic. Locally grown."

Nero huffed.

The Angel shot to his feet. "I'll get you some. You can stay for as long as you want. It's kind of boring being in this giant place by myself. I leave every few days to get food but that's about all the excitement in my life." The Angel strode to the kitchen and got two carrots from the fridge. He returned to where Nero was resting, but the horse was asleep.

The Angel set the carrots next to Nero and moved to a nearby chair.

When Nero woke in the morning, he was greeted by a naked Angel sipping coffee in a club chair and reading a romance novel.

Nero nickered in disgust.

"Look, bro, I've been here for a few days now and I'm just enjoying the freedoms of the Earthen plane." He snuggled down in the chair and threw a blanket over his lap. "Nudity in Heaven is unheard of. Probably because it feels so nice to be naked." He pointed down the hall that led to the bedrooms. "I'm pretty sure your room is down there. One specifically smelled like a barn stall."

Nero showed his teeth and snapped them together in warning before moving to his feet and walking down the hall to his room. He nudged the door open and was greeted by the familiar scene. This was the room Jed had designed for him. A comfortable bed, plenty of space. He looked toward the bathroom. There probably wasn't fresh water in the tub. Nero settled down for a few more hours sleep and thought of Shay, hoping that she was okay and safe.

# Thirteen

*Meg*

MY STOMACH GROWLS, echoing throughout the main room of the Safe House. Something hears it and I curse my body for requiring food and blood so frequently. There are shuffling footsteps from deep in the Safe House. I pick up my pace and get the heck out of there.

Stepping outside, a strange sense of tension lifts from my shoulders. I walk closer to the street signs, patting my pocket. There was a portal in a graveyard not far from here. An arrow points to Owasco Lake. Water is a universal conduit, the Scarecrow once told me. If there's water, I can whisper a little rhyme and I could use the lake to make it back to the Seven Kingdoms of Heaven. It would definitely be faster than trucking it all the way to the graveyard.

I follow the signage to Owasco Lake and start walking down West Garden Street. There are hotels on each side of the street and big parking lots with potholes and crumbling asphalt. I keep my blade in my hand, ready to take on trouble. There's a sign for Holy Family Catholic Church and I notice the walking dead milling about in the parking lot. Maybe they're waiting for mass?

I move behind some broken down cars and keep moving. As the sun lights Hellsky, I make good time. I take West Garden Street until it comes to a dead end, then turn onto North Street and make my way to Osborne Street then East Genesee Street, then follow the sign pointing to Owasco Street. The lake is one mile away. I could run it in about nine minutes if I can still live up to my old high school mile run time. I didn't have to drag a broken wing on my back so I decide to take my time. The dead keep their distance and a sign for Fine Food and Gas catches my attention. My stomach grumbles again. My mouth waters at the thought of Hostess cupcakes and sugary soda. I smooth my hand over the feather in my pocket. I haven't eaten a real meal since that sandwich earlier. My gaze lingers on the gas station. The windows aren't broken and the door isn't chained, I can see the plastic packaging reflecting the morning light. It hasn't been twenty-four hours. I have time to get a snack.

I open the door to the shop slowly, reaching up with my blade and silencing the bell that would announce my arrival. The fluorescent lights flicker, casting a sickly pallor over the shelves of snacks and the grimy floor. My stomach growls as I take in the rows of chips and candy. I grab two packs of chocolate cupcakes and a pack of Snowballs. I linger in the aisle, opening one of cupcakes and shoving it whole into my mouth. I grab a Kit-Kat bar and tuck it into the side pocket of my backpack for later.

I gaze at the drink selection. I should choose a water but lemon-lime soda grabs my attention. I open a bottle and wash down the cupcake. I reach for another and tuck it under my arm. I'm almost done here, why not be greedy? I doubt where ever I go next they'll have snacks like this. I take another package of Snowballs and head toward the door.

As I pass the counter, I feel a prickle of unease crawl up my spine. I turn, scanning the shadows in the back of the store but see nothing out of the ordinary.

I shove another cupcake in my mouth and push open the door. The moment I step outside, the air seems to thicken, becoming heavy and oppressive. I barely have time to react before Alastor and his Hellions emerge from a two black Jeeps. I stumble, shocked. I didn't even hear them pull up. Their eyes are gleaming with malice.

"Going somewhere, Meg?" Alastor sneers, his voice dripping with contempt.

The Demon looks like absolute dog shit. The throne does not look good on him. His clothing is disheveled, his hair messy and knotted. There's blood dried to his chin which tells me he's been drinking blood like a slob. I glance at his Hellions. Double shit, they look feral, which means they've been drinking fresh blood.

My heart pounds against my ribs as I flex my wings, desperate to fly away and divebomb into the lake in the distance.

Alastor glances at the packages in my arms.

"You were supposed to be finding Lucifer's bones, not shopping," he grumbles.

"Sorry." My eyes widen. "But," I clear my throat, "they're not here."

"Where have you been?" Alastor asks.

"Staving off death after you fed me that blood from the dead, dickhead." I'm not giving him any details, definitely not telling him that Sparrow had me locked up in Heaven until the rotten blood was out of my system.

Alastor glares at me as his Hellions pace like guard dogs. "What must I do to make you bring me those bones?" he asks.

"I'm clearly searching for them."

"You're shopping at a snack shop." Alastor points to the Hostess snacks in my arms.

"Fine," I lift my arms and everything falls to the ground. "I was hungry but I'll stop. I'll be on my way."

The soda bottle cracks and fizzles against the pavement, along with my hopes for making it to the lake and escaping.

"This is no game," Alastor says, his smile widening. "This is justice for Lucifer."

The Hellions lunge at me. I sidestep out of their reach. But a big one with a face like a boar grabs me. I punch his arm and kick his shin. I fight back with every ounce of strength I have left. My fist connects with demonic flesh. I grip my blade and slice one across the chest, then backstep to put distance between us. I didn't come into this fight at a hundred percent. One throws a fist that lands directly in my gut, sending me flying. I land on my back and hear the Kit-Kat bar snap like my last fuck.

That's it. I scramble to my feet and swing my blade, cutting off an arm. While that Hellion grumbles, I launch myself into the air and try to fly. With only one functioning wing, it's just enough rise to get a few stories up before they come after me.

We tangle in the air but I'm no match like this. One grabs onto my pack. I cut the strap and let it fall. Then I drop to the ground and roll to get out of their way. One grabs me by the throat and slams me against the wall of the store. Bone scrapes against brick wall and I hold in a hiss on discomfort. Nope, it's not a Hellion, it's Alastor.

"You've caused me enough trouble," he hisses, his face inches from mine. "Take me to the bones. Now."

"I've been searching, I don't know where they are."

"I don't believe you. What are you doing out here?" he slams me against the wall, harder this time.

"Checking the Auburn Safe House," I say. "Or what's left of it."

He looks down my frame to my boots and my blade. "Interesting."

He punches me in the jaw and I see stars before I can stab him in the gut.

"I'll tell you something, Meg." His grip loosens on my throat. "I think you're up to no good. I think you're being sneaky." He throws me on the ground. "I think you might have help. Where's that old Hellion I left you with?"

"Dead," I groan.

Alastor kicks me over onto my stomach. "And where are the chains?"

I don't say anything because I can't really think of a lie that would make sense.

His boot slams down on my spine, right between my shoulders.

"Tell me, Fallen Queen. Tell me the truth." He pauses

and I hear what sounds like his head shaking. "Shut up!" he screams. "Shut up. Shut up. Shut up!" he slaps the side of his head.

"Are you fucked in the head?" I ask. "I used to know someone like that. It never ends well."

He drops to the ground, knees on each side of my back. "Those Archangels always said you had a fucking rich mouth. I'll give you something to flap your lips about."

The metallic zing of knife leaving its sheath echoes against the brick wall to my right. I struggle, trying to throw him off my back but he's too big.

"Hold down her arms," Alastor shouts to his Hellions.

Claws grip my wrists and pull my arms taut.

Hot breath brushes my face as he whispers, "Heard it took ages for you to get these."

I scream as he pulls my broken wing out straight. Bone rubs against the ground but it's nothing compared to the searing pain of his blade slicing through the thick tendons and bone of where my wings come out of my back. He cuts and saws with a serrated blade, slicing through my wing. Agony unlike anything I've ever known tears through me. I scream, the sound echoing through the empty streets as he cuts off the second wing. I scream, thinking it will never end. My voice echoes off the brick walls and my ears ring from the escalating sound of it.

I lay there, gasping for breath, my vision blurring from the pain.

Alastor moves to his feet, looming over me, his Hellions flanking him. "I'll leave you to die here," he says, ice in his voice. "Consider it mercy. Tell me where his bones are!" Alastor spits the words at me.

I press my lips together and hold in a cry of anguish. It hurts so bad. Blood is pouring down my sides, pooling under my chest. Through blurry vision, I recognize my lifeless wings on the ground. The Hellions release my wrists and I grip the dirt.

"Fine. Have it your way." Alastor picks up my wings and walks away, dragging them like palm fronds. "When you wake, bring me the bones. This is my last request. The next time I draw a blade on you, it will be to cut off your head."

As they walk away, I try to move, but every part of me feels shattered. This is worse than that day I killed those seven men. Worse than the day Sparrow stabbed me in the heart. Worse than anything. Darkness creeps in at the edges of my vision, and I can only hope that someone, anyone—maybe even Sparrow—might find me before it's too late.

# FOURTEEN

*THEN*

"SPARROW!" Meg called.

Sparrow was inspecting the burned ruins of his home. He'd returned to nothing, just ash and bone and sorrow. He'd been on the dark side of the walking dead for most of it. Meg had locked him up in the dungeon to keep him safe and figure out a way to cure him from the zombie bite on his leg. His ankle itched and he had a memory of Teari telling Meg to cut his leg off to stop the spread of the dead. She refused, thankfully. Part of him felt hollow for not fighting during the war. He spent his whole life training and preparing for battle, and he spent the time behind bars thinking of eating flesh. He was quite worthless for the whole ordeal.

The Archangel at his side wouldn't stop talking. "Your sister perished in the war alongside her husband."

It took Sparrow minutes to process what the man had said. Nightingale was gone. Jack was gone. He didn't mention the baby.

"What happened to their son, Thrush?"

"Can't find him. Either he perished by the Basilisk or that blasphemous trash from Hell took him. She was here. She brought the fast-dead. She brought the Basilisk. She brought death upon your family."

Sparrow glared at the Archangel, searching for truth. Angels couldn't lie but they could deceive. They could spread misinformation if they didn't know any better or if they chose to believe untruth.

"You must put an end to her. Purify your blood. You must set everything right again."

Sparrow tried to process everything but his brain was working in slow motion.

"You must do this to take your family's kingdom," the Archangel said. "You have to rid yourself of her filth. You are pure blood, your heritage cannot be tainted."

"She's half and half," Sparrow said, guilt and longing overriding everything. He rubbed his head, trying to rationalize what was right and what was wrong, what was true and what was deception.

"The rules of the Seven Kingdoms of Heaven are clear. You have seen darkness, you have seen light, you have been *tainted*. As long as your blood flows through *her* veins, you cannot take this land. You will not find peace. Your blood lineage does not need any more curses."

Sparrow glanced at Meg as Clea's omen ran through his mind.

. . .

*Wars. Blood and death. Good and evil. A dead Sparrow. A motherless child and a fatherless child. Light and dark. The Earthen plane and the ethereal realms. A burst of bright light. An explosion. Fear and pain. Emptiness. A dark, never-ending vat of emptiness that would suck every joyful moment right out of me.*

*"I saw a dark future, one where we are separate," Sparrow had told Meg.*

"You will lose everything. Your family, your lands, your namesake. After all you've been through you can't walk away from your family throne." The Archangel said as he passed a knife into Sparrow's hand. "Straight through into the heart. If you don't do it, I will kill her where she stands. This is for your own good. For the good of Babylon. For the good of balance between realms."

"Sparrow," Meg called. "Will you talk to me?" Her voice sounded innocent, hopeful.

Sparrow took the knife. Grief gripped his chest. He didn't want it to end like this. He never wanted this. Damn he missed her, foul mouth and all.

Sparrow considered the first moment he'd seen Meg and lost her. He considered that lifetime banishment would have been better than this. He wasn't sure how they found each other in Noah's basement all those years ago, but with the task he now faced, he wished he'd never knocked on that door. He wished he'd wandered Hellscape alone into oblivion. Too many had intervened into their relationship.

There's joy on her face.

His heart shreds.

"Sparrow," Meg said. "You're back. "You're you." She smiled, hope lighting her face.

This was all they ever wanted. Freedom.

The blood running through his veins was like ice water. He had to play the part, to make it easier for her. The only way she'd survive this was on pure unadulterated hate for him.

"Is that so?" Sparrow's voice sounded strange to his own ears.

He revealed the knife, and she saw the glint of sun on the blade. Teari's blood had given him strength, more than his years of training as Legion Commander and Hellion leader. He moved quickly and threw jabs to distract the Archangel and make him believe Sparrow wasn't holding back. Three to the stomach, to prevent any seed from taking. One to her thigh that he'd miss wrapping around his body. One to the arm that would never embrace his shoulders ever again. He held the blade against her breastbone. He had to do this. Had to. He hated himself for it.

She was pale with shock and pain.

He was the worst thing to ever walk the realms. A creature of death. A horrible creature that could never be trusted. Sparrow told himself what he was. He could have killed the Archangel and embraced the chaos. But then they'd never be free of this dance. This is what they needed, *freedom*. And there was only freedom in death and the spilling of blood.

"An eye for an eye. Grace for grace," Sparrow's voice was malevolent, filled with hatred. He'd never heard his voice like that. It was hatred for what they'd been through. Hatred for the laws of Babylon. It was all wrong. "Except you never had a speck of grace. I'll have to take something else."

He gazed into her blue eyes and saw the torture she'd endured at his hand. It was unexpected for them both. He would always hate himself for this moment. He hoped she'd hate him forever because there was nothing he could do to mend the sharp edge of betrayal.

He pushed the blade into her breast bone, past the cartilage, into the firm muscle of her heart. He glanced down, saw the blade was embedded in her watercolor tattoo of a sparrow in flight.

He couldn't explain the look on her face but he knew it was all he'd ever see for the rest of his life. It would haunt him forever.

*Poof* – she disappeared.

"Where did she go?" the Archangel asked.

"What does it matter? I did what you asked, now get off my land." Sparrow took in the scene–the rubble and the rotting basilisk carcass were all that remained of his father's house.

"You can rebuild." The Archangel was examining. "You'll need more souls since your kingdom lost nearly everything in the Fast-Zombie War. Congratulations on inheriting the weakest kingdom in the Seven Kingdoms of Heaven."

Rock bottom wasn't new to Sparrow. He just didn't expect the void within his center to be so deep. He had a dream of taking over these lands with Meg at his side. Now that would never be. He threw the bloody knife into the soil at the Archangel's feet.

*"I saw a dark future, one where we are separate."*

# Fifteen

Sparrow moved cautiously through the darkened halls of the castle in the burning caves. His footsteps echoed against the cold stone floors. The oppressive atmosphere of the place, with its flickering torches casting eerie shadows, did little to calm his nerves. It had been twenty four hours and Meg hadn't returned. He hated himself for not leaving sooner, but he had to gain her trust somehow. He had to live up to his promises. Sparrow kept his expression neutral, hiding the unease that twisted in his gut as he approached the imposing doors to the ballroom which had become Alastor's chamber. He could smell the Demon from here.

With a steady hand, Sparrow pushed the heavy door open and stepped inside. Alastor was pacing near the balcony, stroking his chest pocket as though something beloved lay inside.

Alastor's eyes flicked to meet Sparrow's with a mixture of curiosity and suspicion.

"Raven King," Alastor greeted, his voice a low rumble.

"To what do I owe the pleasure? Have you found Meg yet?" The last question was delivered with a sly smile and narrowing of dark eyes.

"Just checking in before I start my searching for today." Sparrow forced a smile, masking his true intentions.

"Just checking in," Alastor mimicked.

As Sparrow scanned the room, his eyes fell upon something that made his blood run cold. Mounted on the wall behind Alastor's club chair, were a pair of familiar, mottled brown wings. Meg's wings. His heart thrummed against his ribs but he kept his composure and held in every ounce of reaction.

Alastor followed Sparrow's stare and chuckled darkly. "Ah, those. A little souvenir from our dear Meg. Seems you're not very good at hide and seek. I found her this morning."

Sparrow clenched his fists, every muscle in his body tensing. "Babylon still wants her soul. You bastard," he spat, the fury barely contained.

Alastor walked closer, the smirk never leaving his face. "Careful, Raven King. You wouldn't want to be caught double-crossing me, would you? I've been hearing whispers that you've been less than loyal."

Sparrow took a step forward, his eyes blazing and hand hovering over his blade. "I owe no loyalty to you, bastard princeling. I hold no loyalty to a *seat holder*."

"*Kill him. Kill him. Kill him.*" Lucifer's voice screamed in Alastor's mind.

"If you ever want to be free of your father, you should tread lightly around matters of Meg." Sparrow's eyes were blazing as he handed down the warning.

Alastor laughed, the sound devoid of any warmth. "Bold words from a King who has dabbled in darkness. Remember, Sparrow, I hold the power here. Step out of line and you'll end up just like those wings on my wall."

Alastor muttered something in Hellspeak and the ground cracked under his feet. Bugs and snakes and small Demons began crawling out.

Sparrow ran, leapt into the air, and twisted his body so his shoulder hit the glass window, breaking it. Glass shattered and rained down over the ballroom. He kicked off the frame and took to the air. Black wings spread wide, propelling the shards of glass back at Alastor.

"You're running?" Alastor shouted at him. "After all this?"

"This isn't running," Sparrow shouted back. "There is more at play than your simple chore of finding Lucifer's bones. You have caused chaos between the realms. Now I must clean up your filth." Sparrow flew closer. "And don't forget, you're still behind on your soul quota. We have a deal." Sparrow hovered in the air, pointing his blade in Alastor's direction. "Where is she?"

Something clicked in Alastor's gaze. The poor bastard. He had very limited control of his own mind. It wasn't enough to forgive, Sparrow would never trust the Demon even after he was free of Lucifer.

"Tell me now!" Sparrow shouted.

Alastor pointed to the North. "She's near the Auburn Safe House. If the dead haven't eaten her yet."

———

The Raven King took to the sky. He was a dark shadow that passed over the land of Hell. The Auburn Safe House was far and it would take him hours to get there. Each beat of his wings felt like a hammering reminder of urgency, pushing him forward. The hours passed by quickly, determination keeping him aloft and he cursed himself the entire way for letting her go alone. He knew she wouldn't allow him to go with her. He'd be more of a distraction than anything. They'd fight the entire time. She'd try to kill him and he'd be fighting himself not to spill the truth. The court of Babylon would be suspicious. He couldn't have risked it.

Sparrow scanned the barren landscape below, eyes sharp despite the weariness that gnawed at his muscles. Hellscape sprawled beneath him, a desolate wasteland spattered with hordes of the walking dead. Newly dead souls ran for cover when they saw his shadow pass over. He had to find her, quickly. The thought of Meg lying somewhere, injured and alone, spurred him on.

After what felt like an eternity, he spotted a dark silhouette sprawled on the ground. Darkness stained the space around her, spread out like wings of blood. His heart lurched as he descended rapidly, the coppery scent hitting him before his feet touched ground.

"No." His voice cracked with desperation. "No. No." Sparrow dropped to his knees. There was so much blood. Too much blood. She was laying on her stomach, the bloody stems of her wings leaking and saturating his pants. Dark hair covered her face.

Meg's eyes flickered open, a faint smile curved her lips

despite the pain etched into her features. "Raven King," she whispered, voice barely audible. "You found me."

He never deserved her smile. She must be so close to death she couldn't remember her hate for him.

Sparrow gently cradled her body, trying to stem the flow of blood with trembling hands. The realization of her injuries crashed over him like a tidal wave, but he forced himself to stay calm even though his gut twisted. There was no time for panic. No time to think of what Gabriel would do to him. No time to think of Babylon's disappointment if she died.

She needed blood. Badly. "Tell me who you are bonded to," Sparrow demanded.

"I'll never tell you," Meg whispered.

"Tell me who holds the blood bond," Sparrow said. "I'll go get them. I'll find them. Tell me now."

Meg pressed her lips together. She seemed content with death.

"Christ, Meg, you're not going to make it."

She saw the glimmer of fear behind his steely gaze.

"Who?" he asked again.

She looked away from him. "There is no one. I haven't had a blood bond since Skeele died." Meg's throat felt thick and dry, her head full. Her vision was doubled and she closed her eyes because the sensation felt strange.

"Fuck." Sparrow moved to his feet and paced, tore his hands through his hair. The edges of his wings made a *shhhh* sound as they dragged against the pavement. It was soothing, making Meg want to fall asleep; a lullaby of feathers scraping. Meg closed her eyes, her body shutting down. She remembered this feeling, she'd felt it more than once, but there was always the warm press of Skeele's wrist to her lips to bring her back to life.

"Meg, can you hear me?" A swipe of blood stained his chin. He kneeled next to her again. He slapped her cheek lightly but she didn't respond. Not even a moan. She was pale as a ghost. "Wake up." He shook her harder.

She didn't rouse.

Sparrow turned her body and not even the discomfort of her wounds pressing against the pavement brought a flinch to her face. There was one thing he could do. One thing that would save her. One thing that would cause her to hate him forever.

"Give me permission," he begged. Sparrow didn't want to do this against her will but he was running out of options. Although, he didn't ask her permission before stabbing her. "Meg, tell me yes." He was running out of time. Fuck it. Fangs. He tore his own wrist before pressing it to her mouth.

Sparrow's blood dripped between her lips and down her throat. She was going to fucking kill him for this. Because now, they wouldn't be able to escape each other. Now they'd be blood bonded. Again.

# SIXTEEN

THRUSH TORE THROUGH THE DRAWERS OF THE small cottage, his movements frantic and agitated. He was on a mission to find scissors. His body ached, his muscles ached, but worse was the damn white-blonde hair that kept falling into his eyes as his uncle's Legion beat him to a pulp every day under the guise of teaching him something. Everything felt out of control, and he desperately needed to change something – anything. His hair had grown unruly, a wild mess, just like his chaotic life. He needed to cut it, he needed some control.

Nightingale and Noah entered the cottage, sensing the tension even before they saw their son.

"Thrush, what are you doing?" Nightingale asked with a soft whistle, her voice filled with concern.

"Looking for scissors," Thrush snapped, slamming another drawer shut. "I need to cut this damn hair."

Noah stepped forward, his expression stern. "Thrush, calm down. Talk to us."

"There's nothing to talk about," Thrush shot back, his

eyes blazing with frustration. "I can't go back to Hell. I won't. I hate that we're all scattered, that my friends are suffering, maybe even dead, who knows... and I'm stuck here."

Nightingale sighed, reaching out to touch his shoulder. "We know it's hard, but running away from your duties won't help. You are part of a bigger plan." She lowered her gaze. "If you don't do your time as a Hellion, the family curse will return. You don't want that on your shoulders."

Thrush pulled away from her touch, his anger palpable. "I never asked to be part of this *plan*. I don't care about some obscure rules between the realms. I just want my life back. If there is no one else to curse, what does it matter?"

"If you have children–" Nightingale started to say.

"I'd never bring a kid into this mess," Thrush spat.

Noah handed Thrush a pair of scissors he'd found. "If cutting your hair makes you feel better, do it. But know that it won't change what you must face."

Thrush grabbed the scissors and moved to a mirror. With determined snips, he started cutting away chunks of hair, the pieces falling to the floor like snow. Nightingale stepped closer, gently taking the scissors from him and evening out his haphazard work. "I used to do this when you were a baby," she said softly. "Until you made me stop. You're not alone in this," she whispered, her hands steady as she trimmed his hair shorter. "We all have our battles, Thrush. But we face them together."

"We shouldn't be here." Thrush scowled. "We should be helping Meg. We should be with Remington and Rue. We shouldn't be separated."

"I miss them too," Noah said.

After a tense silence, Thrush pulled away from Nightingale and stormed out of the cottage.

"I'll go after him," Noah said.

"Please," Nightingale whispered, bending to scoop up the hair on the floor. It sifted through her fingers like snow.

Noah followed Thrush, the two walking toward the practice grounds. "I'll never get over this freaking sun." Noah pulled a pair of sunglasses out of his pocket and put them on. "Thrush, I understand you're upset. But avoiding responsibilities won't help."

Thrush scoffed. "You don't get it, Dad. I don't want to be a Hellion. I don't want to learn darkness." He used air-quotes as he mimicked Sparrow's words. "I miss my friends and I hate that we are all split up."

Noah placed a hand on Thrush's shoulder, squeezing gently. "It'll be okay. We'll find a way through this. But you have to trust us, trust the rules of the realms."

Thrush scoffed. "Yeah, like you and Mom? Following rules got you both killed."

"Hey," Noah tugged on Thrush's arm. "I died on the way to prison. And your mom died protecting you."

"I don't want to talk about this anymore," Thrush said as he stumbled to a standstill. "Holy shit."

Both were stopped in their tracks by a chilling sight. Sparrow, exhausted and distraught, was carrying Meg's limp body. Her wings were gone, her form lifeless and bloodied. Sparrow's pants were saturated in blood. Smoke rose from their bodies and the scent of brimstone wafted in the slight breeze.

"Oh my God." Noah ran toward them. "What happened?" he demanded, rushing to help.

Sparrow's eyes were hollow, filled with a mixture of rage and disappointment. "Alastor happened. We need to get her inside."

Thrush felt his stomach drop, the anger inside him turning to ice-cold fear. "Is she..."

"She's alive," Sparrow said through gritted teeth. "But barely. We need to move, now."

Noah ran forward and opened the door to the main house.

"Don't you have somewhere to be?" Sparrow snapped at Thrush. "Go!"

"We'll catch up later," Noah said, motioning for Thrush to head to training.

"There's an empty room in the back of the house," Sparrow nodded the direction so Noah could clear the way.

Meg's blood left a trail, dripping onto hardwood floors and smearing on the walls as Sparrow carried her.

Noah opened the door to the bedroom and pulled back the sheets.

"Get towels from the bathroom," Sparrow said.

Noah grabbed a stack from the bathroom closet and laid them out on the bed. "Do you have a healer I should call on?" Noah asked.

"I don't have a healer." Sparrow settled Meg on the bed and turned her so she was laying on her stomach.

"Christ." Noah rubbed his face, turned pale as dread threaded his veins. "Her wings."

"Get some water," Sparrow ordered, reaching for the hem of her shirt and tearing it off.

"You should get a healer in here to help." Noah said from the bathroom.

"I said I don't have one."

"Don't you have friends? Call Teari." Something fell on the floor.

Sparrow dabbed at the oozing bone. "She's not really my friend."

"Well maybe you should be nicer to her. To everyone." Noah walked into the room with cloths and a wash bin of water. "You won't get far without friends."

"She'll live," Sparrow muttered as he cleaned Meg's back. Dried blood and dirt were crusted to her skin.

"How can you be so certain?" Noah asked, picking up a cloth and scrubbing. "I'm really tired of seeing one of my best friends nearly dead."

Sparrow paused for too long. "She's breathing." He motioned to the slight expansion of her rib cage.

"You have blood here?" Noah asked. "Blood would help her heal." He rubbed his face. "Last time she was injured like this, Teari said use blood from someone who had a bond with her." A million thoughts ran through Noah's mind and his hand that was cleaning her slowed. Everyone close to her was gone.

"She's had some already." Sparrow rinsed the cloth and resumed cleaning the red skin surrounding the bony protrusions.

"You found Skeele?"

"Skeele died weeks ago," Sparrow said.

Noah stopped washing her shoulder and stared at Sparrow, then glanced at the healing wound to Sparrow's wrist. "Please tell me you didn't do what I think you did."

Sparrow pressed his lips together in a straight line. "I didn't do it."

"Liar."

"I can't lie, I'm an Angel."

"No," Noah chuckled. "You're definitely not an Angel. You're not like the others. The rules don't seem to apply. I know a good liar when I see one. Meg's been my best friend for a long time." Noah pointed at the Raven King. "Angels can't lie, they can deceive. But you straight up lied to me just now. Liar, liar, pants on fire."

Sparrow muttered something about ghosts minding their own business and stupid child songs.

"Meg is my business." Noah picked up the wash bin and took it to the bathroom to get fresh water.

Sparrow kneeled next to the bed and continued cleaning blood off Meg. Her arm was hanging off the side of the bed and her face was relaxed in sleep.

Noah would never forget the scene; the way the Raven King looked kneeling beside a half-dead Meg, the look on his face, the emotion in the room, the tension, the knowledge that she'd live but they'd all have to deal with the repercussions of how Sparrow had saved her.

Noah set the wash bin down and water splashed. "Who else knows?" he asked.

"No one. As soon as I found her, I brought her directly here."

Noah and Sparrow cleaned her skin and dressed her wounds.

"Nightingale is going to want to see her," Noah said. "I can't keep this from her. You know she's been asking."

Sparrow nodded. "I know. Just... give me a few minutes."

Noah left the room with dueling emotions. He was glad

to see Meg, but worried that Sparrow had clearly blood bonded with her after everything. He wasn't so sure Meg's heart could handle another blow.

She'd want to see her children. And judging from the clipped conversation with Sparrow, Noah assumed the war in Hell was far from over.

# SEVENTEEN

*MEG*

I OPEN my eyes to a blur of darkness. My entire body aches, heavy with exhaustion and pain. I blink a few times, clearing the sleep. Panic surges through me as I try to move, a sharp, agonizing pain shooting through my back. It takes a moment for reality to sink in... my wings are gone.

"I'm sorry he took your wings," Nightingale's voice is soft. "It's not right."

"It doesn't matter. I've lived more of my life without them than with them. Where am I, Night?"

"Somewhere safe. Go back to sleep," she says.

"I don't want to sleep," I mutter. "Been sleeping for too long."

But my eyelids are so heavy I can't keep them open.

---

*I TASTE blood in my mouth. Fresh, sweet, tangy. A sensation in my core throbs and burns. The images behind my eyes are nothing short of pornographic. A blurry face, his mouth on me; sucking, licking, fingers probing. Christ. I roll my hips, lick my lips. The blood stops flowing. The dream dissipates to darkness.*

———

"GET UP, MEG," Nightingale's voice pierces through the fog in my brain. Her tone is urgent, laced with an edge of desperation. "You need to get up."

My eyes flutter open. I feel better–still tired but I can move my arms. I turn my head slowly, wincing with the effort.

"How long have I been sleeping?" I ask.

"About two days." I hear the familiar sound of Nightingale's roller skates as she comes closer. "You need to get up. Babylon wants to meet with you." Nightingale's face appears as she leans over me. "Come on, get out of bed." She grips my arms and helps me move.

"Why are you so bossy?" I ask, doing my best to ignore the sharp ache in my back as I sit up.

"Are you dizzy?" she asks.

"I don't think so."

"Good. You need to wash your hair. You stink." There's concern in her eyes. "The Queen of Hell can't be looking like this."

"I am no longer the Queen of Hell. Wait..." I go still as I piece together what she's said. "If you're here then I'm in Sparrow's Kingdom, again."

"Again?" Nightingale asks. "You haven't been here in ages."

"I was here before. Babylon sent me to get the feather of truth in Hell."

Nightingale's face twists in realization. "That bastard." Her hands clench to fists.

I don't argue with her. I can't; my mind is racing, trying to make sense of what happened. Alastor. The snack shop. The attack. Busted Kit-Kat bar. The feel of my wings being severed from my body.

"My... my wings," I choke out, my hands trembling as I reach over my shoulder to touch the bandaged stumps. A sharp ache radiates and my fingers snap away. "I'm useless."

"Don't say that," Nightingale snaps, her grip on my arms tightening. "You are not useless, Meg. You are strong." She bends to look into my eyes. "You can do this."

Somewhere deep inside, I know she's right. I have to keep fighting if my children will ever see peace. I can't give up.

"This sucks donkey balls," I say, my voice barely more than a whisper.

"Probably," Night agrees. "We must get you moving. Get up, get dressed." She steadies my arm as I move upright. "Thrush will be done with training soon. He wants to see you. He's worried."

"Okay." I nod.

Drawing on every ounce of strength I have left, I grab Nightingale's arm and try to stand. The pain is unbearable but with her support, I manage to get to my feet. I sway, my vision swimming.

"That's it," Nightingale encourages me.

I nod, clinging to her words like a lifeline. One step at a time. I can do this. I must do this.

Nightingale helps me wash my hair and get the rest of my body clean. She appears with my bugout bag, the straps cut and covered in dirt and blood. "You have clothes in here?" she asks.

I nod as I dry myself and run my fingers through my hair. She digs through the bag and finds clean clothing.

"This is all you've got," she says setting the clothes on the countertop. "We'll get you looking right and maybe Teari will bless us with her good graces and offer you some pain relief."

I reach for my pack, unzip the front pocket, and pull out the smashed Kit-Kat. I rip open the package and eat the busted pieces that are big enough to pick up. If I could, I'd lick the package. My stomach growls and Nightingale notices.

"We'll get you something to eat. The kitchen has really good food." Her eyes narrow in concern as I lick my fingertip then dab the tiny pieces of chocolate and press them to my tongue.

Nightingale helps me dress, easing my shirt over my back. The slits for my wings allow the bandages to poke through. I finger-comb my hair in the mirror, surprised that Sparrow let me keep it in this room.

"You want to dry it?" Nightingale asks.

"No. Take me to the kitchen." I release the counter and start walking, my legs wobbling.

Nightingale walks me out of the bedroom and down a long hallway to a kitchen. The style of the home is single level, pale colors on the walls, and lots of windows. I only notice two doors in the hall near my bedroom; an open room that looks like it could be a dining room but completely empty, and a living area with a black, overstuffed sectional sofa.

"Here we are," Nightingale says motioning for me to turn.

The kitchen is huge and bright and warm. Nothing in this place reminds me of Remiel's home that was destroyed in the war.

There are fruit and vegetables arranged on an island. Tall chairs line the counter, while a cozy breakfast nook nestles in the corner.

Nightingale helps me to a chair. "I'll get you a plate. What do you want?" she says.

"Everything." It's true, I could eat an ox and an entire restaurant, people included.

Nightingale finds a plate and fills it with premade foods from the fridge. She sets the plate in front of me and I start shoving it all in my mouth. She brings a soda, makes me sandwiches, brings ice cream and cake, chicken wings, pizza. I eat it all but it does nothing to fulfill the *hunger*.

She sits next to me, picks up an apple, and starts eating it.

"Well look what the cat dragged in," a familiar voice says.

"Noah!" I start to move.

"Whoa, whoa, whoa. Stay there." He rounds the island and stands next to me, giving me a side hug as I shove cake in my mouth. "Hungry?"

"Starving," I say around a mouthful.

"Maybe you need something more than regular food."

I pause. "That might be what I need." I haven't had blood since Alastor gave me the rotten blood.

I glance at Noah. He's no longer tethered to me and responsible for finding me food or whatever my heart desires. I look away.

"You don't have to worry," Noah says. "I'll get it." He crosses the room and opens a black fridge in the corner of the room. "Sparrow keeps a stash."

I am reminded of the day I flashed here, stole his blonde girlfriend, and bit her. I'm surprised he doesn't keep women around to feed off. I remember the two closed doors near my room. Maybe he does.

Noah brings me a bag of blood and pours it into a glass.

"I could have just drunk it out of the bag like a Caprisun," I say.

"Nah," he flicks out his pinky finger as he passes me the glass, "this isn't the place to be trashy." He winks, using his entire face to exaggerate it. "You're high class now."

I drink the blood. After, as I'm looking at my empty plate… I'm still hungry. Empty. Like I never ate a thing.

"Maybe I need more." Heat fills my center. I cross my legs and press my thighs together, trying to ignore the ache. Recognition flashes. "Is Skeele still alive?" I ask. "Did someone bring him back to life?" Hope flares in my chest. The image of his death flashes across my vision.

Nightingale shakes her head. "Not that I've heard. I could try searching the Astral realm or his sleep." She offers.

"I don't think so," Noah says. "We would have heard

from him. We would have found him in the Astral," Sparrow said. "He's dead."

I nod and gaze at my empty plate, wishing something would fill the hunger in my stomach. The last time I felt like this I was traipsing through Hell with Sparrow at my side, always hungry because I didn't know blood would fill the hunger.

A sharp intake of breath disrupts the room.

Sparrow is standing in the doorway, staring at me. He looks disheveled, tired, hungry. Something twitches in my center.

"I should go," I mutter, standing.

———

I LAY IN MY BED, watching the curtains blow, remembering the fresh smell of Heaven from the first time I was here. My mind is a haze of pain and worry. I hope Teari comes. I'm not sure how much longer I can deal with the ache across my shoulders.

The door to the room flies open and I turn my head just in time to see Thrush rush in. He's sweating, covered in bruises and dirt. His eyes are wide with concern, his face etched with worry.

"Aunt Meg." Thrush's voice cracks with emotion. He hurries to my bedside and grips me in a tight hug. "I thought you were dead."

"I never stay dead for long." I chuckle. "How are you?" I touch his shoulders then press my hands to his cheeks. "What happened to your hair?"

He points to the sky. "Heaven sun."

I nod. "It looks good. Like a free dye-job. People pay a lot for that on the Earthen plane."

He's staring at me.

"I'm alright," I say, forcing a smile.

"Alright? How can you say that?" he demands. "Look at you. You're hurt. We should be fighting Alastor together, not like this."

I reach out and take his hand, squeezing gently. "I'm stronger than I look. And you... you're doing great out there. Nightingale says you've been training every day. It must be so different from the Hellions though."

Thrush shakes his head vehemently, tears glistening in his eyes. "I don't want to stay in Heaven. It's not home. But I can't go back to Hell either. I don't want to be a Hellion. I can't..."

His words hit me like a punch to the gut. I had always feared a moment like this, the day when the weight of his cursed lineage would bear down on him. The worry wasn't as dire when I sat at the throne. The thought of Thrush succumbing to his family curse, the madness that had plagued Nightingale and Sparrow for generations, terrifies me. And then... there's the thought of others yielding to the curse and suffering.

"Thrush," I say, my voice steady despite the storm of emotions inside me. "I understand how you feel. But running away from it won't make it go away. You have to face it head-on."

"I can't," he whispers, his voice breaking. "What if I end up like... like him?"

"Like who?" I ask.

"Like my uncle, the Raven King... there's nothing worse."

I pull him closer, ignoring the flare of pain across my back. "Listen to me, Thrush. You are stronger than you know. You have a good heart, and that will guide you through the darkest times. You won't end up like him because you have all of us. We're a family, and we'll get through this together."

He buries his face in my shoulder, his body shaking with silent sobs. I hold him as tightly as I can, my own tears emerging.

"Remington and Rue aren't here. We aren't together. I don't like this. It doesn't feel right," Thrush says. "I... I hate it here."

"We will figure this out," I promise. "We'll find a way to make Heaven feel like home. But you have to trust me, Thrush. Trust that this is the right thing to do."

"A long time ago I was here and I hated it too. I felt very wrong being in this place." Memories of waking up in Gabriel's home and attending that party they held to introduce me to the Seven Kingdoms of Heaven flash through my mind. I never felt right here. Not for one moment. "It's going to be okay," I tell him.

Thrush nods against my shoulder, his grip tightening across my shoulders. "I trust you. I just... I don't want to lose myself here."

"You won't," I assure him, my heart aching for the burden he's carried, the burden he will continue to carry. "None of us will let you. We'll find a way."

For a long moment, we stay like this; holding each other, drawing strength from each other. No matter how broken we both feel, as long as we stick together, we can face this. He can face his fate as a Hellion. I'll keep him safe just like the day Nightingale died and I kidnapped him. He may not be my own flesh and blood, but he is Noah's and that just might be closer than family.

# EIGHTEEN

"This is nice," Teari's voice wakes me. "It don't smell like cockroaches in here or nothing." She closes the door then wiggles the handle to make sure it's latched.

"Sure doesn't," I say, sitting up. "You're a sight for sore eyes."

"Why did Sparrow wait so long to ask me to come?" Teari crosses the room and sits on the bed, pulling me close. "He said you nearly died. Again."

"It's not the first time." I shrug. "Look at me now, good as new."

Teari makes a sound as she holds me against her and touches the bandages on my back. "Damn, Meg, this looks awful."

"I can take my shirt off so you can get a better look." I reach for the hem of my shirt.

Teari moves away and waits as I tug it off, moving slowly as I get it over my shoulders then turn my back to her.

"I'm going to take these bandages off," she says.

The tape pulls at my skin as she peels it away. "Oh, Meg," she whispers. "Alastor is a bastard for doing this to you. I'd kill him myself if I had the chance."

"Next time I see him, I will," I promise. "I feel kinda bad for the Demon though, he's losing his mind with whatever Lucifer is doing to him from beyond the grave."

"Must be some kind of possession," Teari says absently as she removes the rest of the bandage. "I feel sorry for all the children of Lucifer. There's a reason why he was the original fallen Archangel."

"Can you fix it?" I ask, looking over my shoulder.

She presses her lips into a frown. "I can't make your wings grow back. But I can smooth the bone and stop it from oozing."

I nod in agreement.

"I'm sorry, Meg," Teari says.

"It's fine. I've lived long enough without them."

Teari rubs her hands together before holding them over my back. I feel the heat and sharp tingle of her healing magic going to work. "Do you want something for the pain?" she asks.

"It doesn't hurt," I lie. I want to remember it. Strength doesn't come from comfort.

"Cutting bone hurts like hell. I don't believe you." Teari's voice holds much concern.

"I can't feel a thing." I think about anything and everything else to distract me from the discomfort and the sound of shards of bone dropping onto the bed behind me. I think of Rue and Remington, Thrush, Sparrow's family curse, and the fact that I must return to Babylon and bring them this damned feather.

Teari's been working for a long time, and my spine aches from sitting upright for her. A cool sensation covers my back.

"I think I'm done here," she says. "Do you want to feel it?"

I reach over my shoulder and she moves my fingers over skin. "You'll have scars and these bony ridges. But it should be more comfortable than how it was."

I can't help the twinge of disappointment as my fingers smooth over the scars.

"I've been told he made you cut off your birthmark," Teari says.

I nod.

"Show me."

I move to take off my pants. There's no shame in her seeing my body, she was there for the birth of my children. I've got nothing to hide from her. Not anymore. If anyone in the Seven Kingdoms of Heaven has my trust, it's Teari. Funny how it didn't start out that way.

She touches the scar on my thigh. "This was the source of you being able to travel like Gabriel?"

"As far as I know."

"Have you tried since it was removed?"

"No."

"Try," she urges.

I close my eyes and channel that power that helped me travel, I repeat the phrase *Angele Dei, illumina, custodi, rege et guberna*. Nothing happens.

"It's not working," I say as I move to get dressed again.

Teari paces the room, thinking. "I don't think this is the end of it all, Meg," she says. "I can find a way to fix this."

"Don't," I say.

"What? Why?"

"The only thing I care about is making sure my children are safe from Remiel's family curse and safe from Lucifer and whomever he decides to possess."

"You're giving up?" she asks. "You're giving up on fighting Alastor?"

"How could I win?" I ask. "I am half of what I was. No wings, no magical ability to travel." I shake my head in disbelief.

"I think you need more time to recover. You've gone through a lot. Losing someone you love and close friends," she sighs. "That's something no one can get over in a few weeks, not after all you've been through. I think you should rest. Take walks and get some sun."

I nod, wishing she'd stop talking.

"Maybe therapy..." she suggests.

"I don't need that. Therapy is for pussies." I lay back, grateful for the lack of ache and pain as I move.

"Consider it, Meg. None of us are immune to sorrow." She looks me up and down as my stomach growls loudly. "You should consider more blood. Probably fresh blood."

I shake my head. "I won't risk a blood bond," I say.

"It will make you stronger," she says.

"I can't risk it." I blink away tears and force my chin to stop quivering. "Never again."

"That's your choice." Something sounds off with the tone of her voice. "Consider eating more meat. Red meat. That might help your hunger. And the bagged blood."

"Sure," I agree.

She collects her bag and steps toward me. "Tell Sparrow

to call for me if you need me again. Don't hesitate. He shouldn't have waited so long." Suddenly, she won't make eye contact.

"Teari..." I start.

"I've got to go. I have an appointment with Gabriel." She seems flustered as she tells me goodbye.

"Are you keeping something from me?" I ask.

"I've got to go." She rushes out the door and her footsteps echo down the hall as she leaves.

I stare at the door to the bedroom. Angels can't lie. They can deceive. But I think Teari just skipped out on the truth by avoidance.

———

Too early in the morning, a knock on my door wakes me.

"Meg," a familiar voice calls. "We must leave."

I open the door and find Sparrow standing there. He takes up the entire doorway, his wings spanning past the decorative casing. He tucks them closer to his back as though he's heard my thoughts. He doesn't look so good. He's pale, bags under his eyes and his cheeks look hollow. He looks... hungry.

"What do you want?" I ask.

"Babylon is calling us. They want the feather," he says. "Get ready." Dull green eyes flash to mine before Sparrow turns and walks away. I'm surprised he shows his back to me like I won't jump on him and slit his throat.

I shove the door closed and get ready.

I open the closet and see the black sweats and few articles of clothing that were in my bag. I need more clothing and instantly miss my closet in Hell. After getting dressed, I open the drawer and pull out the feather of truth. It looks so insignificant to hold so much power. I wonder what Babylon is going to do with it now that all of the Deacons are dead.

I tuck the feather in my pocket and grab my blade. The hall is empty when I open the bedroom door. My stomach growls and I veer toward the kitchen. It's rude that Babylon should call at this unholy hour. There's no time for a real breakfast. I grab fruit and two premade sandwiches. The motor of the black fridge in the corner hums, calling me. I bite a sandwich and cross the room, then pull open the blood fridge. I take out a bag of blood, rip the top with my teeth and down it without taking a breath. I take another bite of sandwich before the feeling of being watched tickles the back of my neck.

Sparrow is standing in the threshold to the kitchen. "Let's go," he orders.

I grab another bag of blood and drink it as I cross the kitchen, throwing the bags in the trash on the way out. I follow up with the next sandwich.

"Are you going to make me walk there again?" I ask.

Sparrow mutters something before saying, "I'm not getting in an enclosed space with you."

"Perfect." I eat the apple next, chewing slowly as he guides me across his property to the walkway under the canopy of trees. I shield my eyes, wishing for sunglasses. I toss the apple core into the bramble.

"Did you bring the feather?" Sparrow asks, his voice dull.

"Of course." I skip a few steps to keep up with him. "Why are we running there?"

"I want to get this over with," Sparrow mutters.

"That makes two of us." I adjust my bag and wish I'd brought more to eat.

We walk in silence and I stare back at the Angels who gawk at us. I flash a sharp smile at a few; they gasp and backstep.

"Stop tormenting them," Sparrow warns. "We're being watched."

"I don't care. I will tear out their necks. I haven't forgotten all they've done." Time can't erase the memory of them taunting me when the Archangels imprisoned me in Babylon. "If I ever find out who threw that tomato at me, I'll cut their arms off."

Sparrow opens the door to the courthouse and holds it for me like I'm a lady or something. It annoys me.

He checks the time as he leads me to the door where the Archangels meet.

"They need another moment," he says, leaning his shoulder against the wall. He looks like he could fall asleep standing.

I nod.

"Did Teari help your back?" he asks.

"Yes. She fixed it the best she could."

Sparrow nods, his eyes drifting over me and it feels like he's imagining me naked standing in front of him.

"What happened here?" Sparrow points to the black, fernlike scars stretching down my arm.

"I was struck by lightning while on the Earthen plane."

"You were cast out." Sparrow's eyes softened.

"Been cast out of plenty of places. They all left scars." I jerk the neck of my shirt down revealing the scar over my heart and the messed-up tattoo. Cast out of a realm, cast out of society, cast out of a heart. It all feels very similar.

Sparrow's mouth opens like he's going to say something but the door to the meeting room opens.

Sparrow enters first.

I follow.

Today the majestic courtroom of Babylon feels particularly oppressive. Golden light filters through the high windows, casting intricate patterns on the marble floors.

Sparrow stands to my right, his presence a mixture of support and silent concern. He doesn't join the rest of the Archangels like before. They watch us, their gaze overwhelming.

Gabriel is the first to speak. He stands, his eyes soft. "Meg, do you have the feather?"

I pull it from my pocket then walk forward and set it on the table.

"We are deeply grateful," Gabriel says. He looks like he wants to say much more but holds it in.

Michael opens his mouth next, his stern face uncharacteristically compassionate. "Your bravery and sacrifice have not gone unnoticed. Your injuries are a testament to the length you've gone for this mission."

"We are truly sorry for the pain you've endured," Raphael says.

I nod. "I'm glad it's over."

Gabriel walks closer and picks up the feather. "We need this, to keep the balance."

Uriel steps forward, his gaze piercing. "Meg, there is one

more task that lies before you. To ensure the balance and prevent further chaos, you must return to Hell and give Alastor the bones of Lucifer."

The room goes silent. A hard chill runs down my spine. I glance at Sparrow, who remains stoic, looking ahead.

"Why me?" I ask. "Why not send someone else?" I scan the table, looking at every one of them. "Why don't you go?" I point at two of them. "Why me? I don't know where his bones are."

Silence.

"I'll go," Sparrow says. "I'll find them."

"No." I shift on my feet. "One of you go." I motion to the Archangels seated before us.

Gabriel sighs, his wings shimmering as he shifts in his seat. He glances at the feather laying on the table in front of him before saying, "Because you're the only one who can get close enough to Alastor. Your previous encounters have given you an understanding of him that none of us possess. And I have it on good accord that you might actually know where his bones are."

"I don't," I say quickly.

"She can't defend herself," Sparrow says.

Rage fills me at the implication of weakness. I tamp it down knowing I'm not what I was. No wings, no magical ability to *poof* and travel at will. I take a shallow breath and choose my next words wisely.

Michael adds, "And because of your unique heritage, you have a resilience that others lack. This mission requires not just strength, but the kind of determination that only you have shown."

Determination to stay alive and keep my children safe. That's all I have determination for these days.

"You found Clea's bones when we'd been searching for *years*," Gabriel says.

I nod, remembering the day I followed the strange inner tug to the location where her bones were buried in a shallow grave. Lucifer is my grandfather though, I'm not sure I could call upon the same power or even succeed.

"We must have balance between the realms," Raphael says. "The Veil is thinning. Chaos will overtake the Earthen plane again. The Fast-Zombie War was devastating. Their souls are trapped in Hell with the Deacons gone."

Sparrow seems strangely calm and impassive during all this.

"You want me to go," I say, the words feeling heavy on my tongue.

"Yes," multiple voices respond.

I clear my throat. "I'll go–"

"You won't go alone this time," Sparrow says again. "I will go, as will others."

"Good," Raphael says.

I raise my hand to interrupt. "I'm only doing this on one condition."

Everyone focuses on me. "Since I could die during this... mission... I want to see my daughter. It could be the last time."

"Where is she?" Raphael asks.

"The Earthen plane. Some place safe." It sickens me to announce what plane they're on.

The Archangels chatter amongst themselves.

"I haven't seen her in months," I say. "I need to see her. I might never see her again."

The strangest thing occurs. I notice Gabriel and Sparrow lock eyes. Sparrow tips his chin in the slightest of nods.

"Yes," Gabriel says before a conclusion is reached between the Archangels. It reminds me that he has held the power in Babylon for a long time with the largest number of souls in his kingdom.

Sparrow and Gabriel keep making eye contact like they're telepathic or have some type of an understanding. Or maybe they're just both fucked in the head for allowing this to go on.

"When?" Gabriel asks.

"Soon," I demand. "Tonight. In the morning. Whenever the portal is free."

"In the morning," Gabriel says. "We'll make sure it's clear for you and Sparrow."

"I don't need a babysitter," I say.

"You won't go alone," Gabriel says.

"Why? Afraid I won't come back?" I ask.

"You have a history of disappearing," Sparrow says.

My head snaps in his direction. The audacity.

"I will return," I promise.

"You can lie," Sparrow says with a smirk.

As we leave the courthouse, Sparrow asks me, "Where are Lucifer's bones?"

I shrug. "I don't know."

He sighs.

I ignore him.

# Nineteen

*Meg*

I JOLT AWAKE, my heart pounding against my ribcage like a drum. *Thump-Thump-Thump*. The room is cloaked in darkness, a sliver of moonlight creeping through the curtains. It takes me a moment to remember where I am—Sparrow's house. The Raven King's prisoner. Heaven. I miss the smell of brimstone. The unfamiliar surroundings add to my disorientation. I shouldn't be here. I don't like that I'm here.

My stomach growls fiercely, the emptiness inside me gnawing with an insistent hunger. I feel like I haven't eaten in days but I remember eating roasted chicken and biscuits and pie before bed. And that bag of blood. Maybe the stress and pain are causing this. Although, the pain has been considerably less since Teari's visit. It could be all the healing catching up with me. My stomach growls again. This hunger is unbearable. I need to eat.

I throw off the covers and swing my legs over the side of the bed, wincing slightly as my feet touch the cool floor. Moving quietly, I navigate through the dark house, moving away from the two doors opposite mine. My footsteps are soft against the wooden planks. I find the kitchen by memory and the faint glow of the moon through the windows.

The kitchen smells like spices and herbs. My eyes adjust to the dim light as I scan the room, searching for something to satisfy the ache in my stomach. It's a bummer, having to find my own food instead of Noah bringing it to me. I open the fridge, grabbing whatever I find—cold cuts, cheese, bread, fruit. I place everything on the counter and start to eat ravenously.

The flavors of each bite burst in my mouth, grounding me to the present moment. The physical act of eating, the taste and texture of the food, it all reminds me that I am still alive, still fighting. And in a few short hours I will see my children. The thought of Sparrow seeing them crosses my mind and bile slides up my throat. I need to escape him. I can't have him go with me.

I move to the pantry, reach for a jar of peanut butter, unscrew the lid, and scoop it out with my fingers. I lick them clean, savoring the creamy sweetness. Next, I devour an apple, crisp and sharp. Tastes like it came from one of the apple orchards near Gouverneur. My stomach growls again, my hunger seeming insatiable, my body demanding more and more. After the apple, I could really go for some pumpkin pie with double whipped cream.

I glance at the black fridge across the room. Blood. No.

Not yet. I press my lips together and hold in the urge to empty the fridge into my gut.

The room is silent except for the sounds of my chewing and the occasional clink of a jar or plate. The darkness feels less oppressive now, the act of eating somehow making everything seem more manageable. I sit at the barstools and lean my elbows on the countertop and take a few deep breaths. Something doesn't feel right. My stomach churns. My throat feels full. A cool sweat breaks out over my skin. Saliva floods my mouth. Christ.

The whisper of feathers dragging against the floor catches my attention. My gaze follows the sound to the threshold of the kitchen. A familiar shadow is standing there, watching silently.

"What do you want?" I ask, fighting the urge to purge everything I've stuffed down my throat the past few minutes.

"I was hungry," Sparrow says. "But it looks like you've eaten me out of house and home."

Gas bubbles up my throat with the burn of stomach acid. I stand, knocking the barstool over. I want to tell him I haven't emptied the blood fridge, but I'm afraid if I open my mouth again, everything I've eaten will be spilled across Sparrow's pristine kitchen floors.

I won't make it back to the bathroom inside my bedroom. I glance around the kitchen, searching for a garbage can. It's been moved. I can't find it. I start opening the lower cabinets, searching for one of those hidden garbage cans. I consider the sink, pausing to hold my stomach.

"What's wrong with you?" he grumbles.

I notice a door to the outside. I conclude I'd rather puke in the bushes than across the floor. I run for the door.

My hand hits cold metal. I shove it open, hearing heavy footsteps following me.

"Don't run, Meg," Sparrow's tired voice echoes across the yard. Sounds like he's not up for a race tonight.

I stumble down two steps, drop to my knees in the grass, and my stomach purges. It must be a scene; the fallen Queen of Hell puking her guts out under the icy moonshine of Heaven.

A bag of blood appears in front of my face, dangling.

"It probably won't hit the spot but it will help," Sparrow says.

I notice a cut on his wrist as I grab at the bag, greedy, and suck it down in a heartbeat. The need to vomit slows but the ache is still there.

"Here," Sparrow says.

I turn and find him holding out another bag of blood for me while he sips from his own. The moonlight is not gentle with his form. He looks gaunt, tired. Dark as a lake. Worse than earlier.

I drink the blood and take a few deep breaths. I should say thank you, but I can't trust opening my mouth again.

I try to move to my feet and Sparrow reaches down, gripping my elbow and helping me up. I don't want him touching me. I should pull away, but I don't.

When I'm on two feet, he steps away like I'm made of lava and might burn his hand. For a moment, I consider death by lava and add it to the list of ways I could kill him.

"Go back to bed, Meg." Sparrow frowns. There is something different in his green eyes. A familiar spark.

"You're not my boss," I argue.

"We have a busy day tomorrow." He finishes his blood but continues to gaze at me.

"Sorry I puked on your grass." I finish my second bag of blood, feeling stronger. I take a few steps away but familiar heat spreads through my lower abdomen. A twinge. An urge. Shit. This blood is not even fresh.

I hold up the bag. "What is this?" I ask.

Sparrow blinks, his head ticks to the side and he shivers. "Go back to bed," he orders through gritted teeth. His wings flash out, shielding the moonlight. It's impressive—always was. The wingspan, the flex of his muscles, the hunger in those green, green eyes. The gaunt stare.

I backstep. A familiar heat floods my core. No. What's wrong with me? Not today Satan. Not today, not ever again.

"What did you give me?" I demand. "What was in that bag?"

"Blood," he spits out. "Now go to bed."

"I am not a child." The scars on my back ache from the urge to spread my wings in an intimidating manner, just like he's doing.

"You are not a child." Sparrow's eyes roam over my body, head to toe, like I'm cake or a rare steak or whatever his favorite food is now.

Fuck.

I turn and reach for the door. A hand slaps down on mine. There is heat and darkness surrounding me. For a moment it feels comforting, like Hell, like... *home*. He twists my hand and the door handle, pulls it open and crowds me until I can feel the barest touch of his chest against my back as he inhales heavy lungfuls of air.

Then his breath is on my ear, stubble scraping against my cheek. I hate myself for not having my blade–it would be the perfect time to slit his throat and drain the blood from his body.

"Go," he demands.

I rip my hand from under his and run inside. I am not what I used to be without wings, without my ability to travel at will, without my blade. I'm nothing more than a weak human right now. Just sharp teeth but I won't risk that. I run through his house and slam my bedroom door closed. I stomp to the bathroom and find my toothbrush, then brush away the taste of vomit with pent up vigor. I could break something or I could fu–

My bedroom door slams open, then closed. I leave the bathroom to investigate. Sparrow is standing just inside my room. His eyes land on mine.

"I shouldn't be here," he whispers. Fists clench. His chin dips and there is something about the way his chest rises and falls.

"You shouldn't." I throw my toothbrush at him and it hits his shoulder then falls to the floor.

Sparrow moves fast as lightning, his hand gliding up the back of my neck then threading into the hair at the base of my skull. He presses his nose to my cheek. He takes a deep breath and closes his eyes. We just stand there for a moment, sharing air, bodies still.

Something dark and hot ignites inside me. "What do you want?" I ask. The room is starting to spin and my knees feel weak.

His eyes flash open and I notice the glint of sharp teeth. A drop of blood sits on his bottom lip.

That familiar ache returns, stronger than ever. I've never been one to make good decisions, or even smart decisions. I'll blame this lapse of judgement on the injuries, the lack of everything right in my life, my humanity. I reach up on my toes and lick the blood off his lower lip. I suck it into my mouth and taste the blood he drank earlier, nip it between my teeth.

A heavy hand falls on my hip and drags me closer.

"I hate you," I remind him. "I will kill you."

"I know." A groan escapes his lips, then a throaty chuckle that makes my insides light with fire. "I love it. Turns me on." And then his mouth is on mine, his tongue dancing in my mouth, hands gripping my flesh and pulling me tighter against his body. He moves to my jaw, then I feel the scrape of teeth over my neck and I tip my head further, a moan escaping my lips.

"Say yes, Meg," he begs. "You must give me permission."

I close my mouth, bite my lips together and refuse, not sure of what I'm giving him permission for. I won't ask his permission when I stab him in the back like he did me.

Sparrow grinds against me, fists gripping my shirt as he rips it down the middle. His hands smooth over my back, stopping at the scars, delicate fingers testing the skin before moving to my neck. Thumbs spread along my jawline and force my head back.

My eyes flash open and I take in his disheveled dark hair, the planes of his handsome face, the torment in his eyes. I wish he would smile. Laugh even. My hands move to the hem of his T-shirt and tug.

Sparrow clicks his tongue. "Tell me," he begs, breathless. He licks my neck, sucks on my collarbone, fingers sliding under the straps of my bra before pushing them away. "Please. Please. Please." He bends to trail kisses down my chest.

I touch him. My fingers slide up the dark marks tattooed on his skin, the tendrils of black that extend up his neck. My fingers slip into his hair as he sets his forehead on my shoulder and twists his head like a big cat being rubbed.

My heart is thudding against my ribs as my hands trail to his front and tug at his shirt, buttons falling to the floor. His touch is both familiar and foreign. Hot and cold. I want his hands on me, but I don't. I want to devour him and I want to slaughter him. There is a war inside my body.

"Meg..." he whispers.

At the sound of my name I am reminded that we shouldn't be here, doing this. But, I fought so hard to have him like this again and failed. Now he's here. What's wrong with one more time? One last time. Can't I finally have what I've wanted, what I've missed, what I've desired for years? Even drowning in heartbreak, I had hoped he'd come back to me. Even filling that emptiness with another, I've always wanted him to come back to me, no matter how much he hurts me. It's a sickness I suppose.

A sickness I fully embrace as I reach for the waistband of his pants.

Here I am, ready to go back to Hell and face my fate. I'm probably going to die for real this time once I hand over Lucifer's bones. I'm going to take one last moment for myself. I'm going to *take* just like the old Meg used to. Take and use and bathe in gluttony.

I push his waistband down and tear his shirt from his shoulders.

He must take it as permission because Sparrow grips me around the waist and throws me onto the bed. He grabs the hem of my pajama pants and tugs them down. His lips brush my ankle, then slide up my leg. He stops at the circular scar where my birthmark once was.

Suddenly I am in a church in Hell...

*SPARROW TURNS, shifting me in his arms. "I didn't hurt you, did I?" he asks, his eyes heavy with concern as he brushes a thumb across my cheek.*

*My throat tightens and something beats heavy in my chest. "No, not even close," I manage to get out, not telling him that sex was never like that, not with anyone, not at any time, ever.*

*He looks down at me, his eyes focused on my tattoos. I suddenly feel self-conscious again.*

*"You don't like them?" I ask.*

*His eyes move to mine and he leans closer to me, pressing his lips to mine. "They're perfect. Just like you." He bends, pressing his lips to the feather across my collarbone. "This one." He rolls me to the side, pressing his lips to the stars on my shoulder. "These." He bends, pressing his lips to the heart on my hip and the anchor on my ribcage. I notice his eyes move lower. "And this one I didn't notice before." His fingers graze the inside of my thigh, up high, almost to where my leg meets my hip, but low enough for it to show when wearing a pair of short shorts.*

*I look down to see his eyes focused on the mark on my upper thigh. "That's not a tattoo," I tell him, my voice sounding thick and abnormal.*

*"It's not?" He sounds distracted, kissing and touching, his fingertips running across my legs, sending a sharp tingle to my lower stomach.*

*"No. It's a birthmark. Daddy always said it was my mark of the devil."*

*"Are you sure that's a birthmark?" he dips his head to inspect the patch of skin that looks like nothing more than an uneven-edged circle.*

*"Yes. Why?"*

*"Because... I think that changes everything." He presses his left thumb to the mark on my thigh, hard, mumbling words in a language I've never heard.*

*A bright white light erupts behind my eyes and a noise that sounds like an air horn fills my ears.*

I shove Sparrow's chest and scoot back from him. "Get away from me," I say.

Sparrow slides back, resting on his knees. His cheeks are flushed but his expression cool. "What?" he asks.

How do I tell him that I'm sad I've lost my ability to *poof* from place to place? I hate that I've lost everything. I finally had a home and now that's gone. I lost my children, my Skeele, my Hellions, my wings. I lost him and now he's here acting like a different person. Like he might actually want me.

Every insecurity I've ever possessed floods me. Teari was right, I need more time.

I pull my knees to my chest and reach for the blanket.

"Get out of here," I say.

Sparrow moves to his feet and... I'm not going to lie, it's impressive the way his abdominal muscles flex and arch, the way his wings drape, the way he crawls and shifts. He turns and walks toward the door without glancing back, without taking his shirt off the floor. When he slams the door closed with the flick of his wrist, I am reminded that I am nothing but his prisoner. I glance around the room and sigh. This is definitely the nicest cell anyone has ever locked me up in. Moonglow glints off the golden door handle. It's not locked. How am I prisoner if it's not locked? I pull the covers over myself and lean against the pillows. Nothing in my life has ever been black and white, it's always been shades of gray.

# TWENTY

The sun was directly overhead, casting a hot glow over the sandy beach. The waves lapped gently at the shore, their rhythmic sound providing a soothing backdrop to the children's laughter. Rue and Remington splashed in the water. Having never been to the beach before, it was easy entertainment for them both. They dove for shells and chased small fish. Remington lifted Rue and tossed her into the waves. Laughter carried on the ocean breeze.

Shay stood a few feet from the water's edge, her arms crossed, eyes scanning the horizon. Chel sat beside her, cross-legged in the sand, looking thoroughly out of place. Jed had gone shopping for food again. Meg hadn't warned them that her children were bottomless pits when it came to food.

"They need this," Shay said, nodding toward the children. "A bit of fun and escape after everything they've been through. It's like a vacation here."

Chel's gaze followed hers, watching. "I agree. But we can't stay here forever. We've been lucky so far."

Shay shook her head. "I think Meg did something to this place. It's so empty. Where else could we go? It's not like we have many options." Shay bent to pick up a seashell. "Maybe a boat on the equator."

"Somewhere the Angels and Demons won't think to look," Chel replied, his tone determined.

"I think you're wrong," Shay said. "I think this place is perfect."

"I just have a bad feeling about it."

Rue and Remington's laughter grew louder and Shay smiled. For a little time, it almost felt like they were just a normal family enjoying a day at the beach. Shay scanned the water line. They were the only family enjoying the beach. They rarely saw another person out here.

"There's something out there," Chel jumped to his feet and pointed.

A gray fin appeared in the water.

A high-pitched scream shattered the peace.

"Rue!" Remington's voice was filled with panic as he swam toward his sister.

Shay and Chel ran into the water, their hearts pounding. Rue was struggling, her face contorted in pain, blood staining the water around her.

"A shark!" Remington shouted, eyes wide with terror and determination as he smashed his fist down on the shark's snout. The creature thrashed, sinking its teeth deeper into Rue's leg.

Shay plunged into the water. Chel was right behind her, his strong arms cutting through the waves.

Remington punched the shark again and again until it released Rue's leg. He gathered Rue under his arm and began dragging her to shore.

Shay and Chel reached the children in seconds. Chel scanned the water for any sign of the shark and saw more fins appearing around the blood trail.

"Get out of the water," Chel shouted. "Now!"

Remington's feet dug into the sand as he ran, dragging his sister along with him.

Shay reached them in seconds. Blood continued to seep from the bite on Rue's leg, mingling with the saltwater.

"Hold on, Rue. We've got you," Shay whispered as she gripped Rue under the arm and helped drag her out of the water.

"Were you bit?" Shay asked Remington, frantically searching him for wounds.

"Just split my knuckles when I punched it." Remington shook his hand as they exited the water.

They moved as quickly as they could, adrenaline propelling them. Remington turned, noticing the blood trail behind them.

As Chel was running toward them, he tore off his shirt and ripped it into strips before dropping to his knees and applying a tourniquet above Rue's knee.

Deep puncture wounds decorated Rue's lower leg. Thankfully, the shark hadn't taken her flesh off the bone.

"Good job," Shay said to Remington. "It could have been a lot worse."

Rue was whimpering in pain. Her face was pale and pinched.

"Let's get her inside," Chel said, lifting Rue into his arms.

Shay grabbed Remington's arm. "Go get Jed."

Remington's eyes went wide. "Alone?" he'd never been sent off alone on the Earthen plane before. Jed and Shay forbid it. The boy never had a moment to himself unless he was in his room or asleep. The idea of going alone was crazy.

"He's not far. Just down the street at the store." Shay gave him a little shove. "Go."

Chel was running with Rue in his arms. Shay ran after him and opened the door to the beach house.

Chel moved inside and set Rue on the island countertop. Shay grabbed clean towels and began creating a makeshift bandage to staunch the bleeding.

"I'll hold pressure on it," Chel said.

Shay's hands trembled as she worked.

"She's going to be okay, Shay."

Shay nodded, her eyes locked on Rue's pale face. "Stay with us, Rue. Just stay with us. Jed will be here soon."

"I...I tried to touch it. I didn't know it would bite me." Rue confessed.

"Why on earth would you try and pet a shark?" Shay asked.

"I've never seen one before. It was curious. It looked friendly." Rue's voice was small. She'd lost a lot of blood and began feeling light headed.

"Sharks never look friendly," Shay said. "Not that I've seen many sharks in Montana, But they never looked friendly in the pictures."

---

REMINGTON LEAPT off the porch and ran, taking a right on Perdido Key Drive. He could see the sign for the Publix grocery store where Jed was shopping.

He flexed his hand, hoping he wasn't dripping blood everywhere. Only two cars passed as he ran, neither seeming concerned about the tattooed teenager running barefoot in boardshorts down the sidewalk.

He was so close. He dug in and ran faster, stopping only to check the road before crossing the street. He ran into the parking lot and noticed the Jeep near the door. Jed was loading bags of groceries in the back.

"Hey. Hey," Remington shouted as he ran up behind Jed.

Jed turned. "Don't sneak up on me like that. You sounded like Nero coming full throttle."

Remington bent and gripped his thighs, taking deep breaths. "It's Rue."

"What happened?" Jed loaded the last bag and slammed the trunk closed.

"She was bit by a shark."

"You have got to be kidding me." Jed's heart plummeted.

"I'm not." Remington's face was pale, tears and sweat dripping down his cheeks. "There's so much blood."

There was blood on Remington's shorts and dripping down his legs, much more than would come from the cuts to his knuckles.

"Get in." Jed pushed the cart away and jumped in the driver's seat.

He peeled out of the parking lot, took a right, and accelerated down the street. He turned left, tires crunching on the narrow, crushed shell road. The Jeep jerked to a stop as Jed threw it in park. The drive had felt like an eternity.

"Get the milk in the fridge," he told Remington as he ran toward the door to the beach house.

Shay and Chel's hands were covered in blood as they held pressure on Rue's leg.

"A shark?" Jed exclaimed, as he slammed the door open.

Rue lay on the island, her leg a bloody mess and her face twisted in pain.

Shay looked up as Jed approached, her eyes filled with desperation. "Jed, please..."

He moved to the opposite side of the counter, his hands hovering over her injured leg. The bite was deep, and the sight of all that blood made his stomach churn. There was no time for hesitation. He took a deep breath, summoning the magic from within him. His hands began to glow with a soft, blue light.

"Hang in there, Rue," Jed murmured, focusing on the wound. Magic flowed from his fingertips, knitting the torn flesh back together, stopping the bleeding.

Rue whimpered, her small hands clutching at the edge of the counter.

"Move the towel," Jed instructed.

Shay pulled it away and tossed it in the sink.

Jed chanted words that sounded like snow falling on rose petals. He poured everything he had into healing her. Slowly, the torn skin and muscle began mending. The glow from Jed's hands faded as the wounds on her leg turned to bright pink skin.

Rue's breathing steadied and she looked up with wide, grateful eyes. "Thank you," she whispered weakly.

"Great job, clotpole," Chel slapped Jed on the back.

Shay's face twisted in confusion.

"Old joke between us," Chel said with a wink.

Jed rested his elbows on the island countertop and bowed his head. "Christ, a shark?"

"It looked friendly," Rue said softly.

"Sharks are never friendly," Jed said.

"I told her that already." Shay reached toward Rue and helped her off the counter. "Go take a shower. I'll bring you clean clothes then we'll have dinner."

Chel helped Remington bring in the remainder of the groceries as Shay cleaned blood off the countertop.

———

As the adults fell into tense conversation, Remington wandered outside. He was looking for Nero, needing someone to talk to. All it took was a few minutes in the ocean to prepare Remington for the fact that they didn't belong on the Earthen plane. There hadn't been any Angel or Demon attacks since they'd arrived, but Rue and Remington didn't know enough about this plane. They didn't know about sharks or other creatures that could harm them. He wandered back to the beach and kicked sand over the trail of Rue's blood. He made it to water, stood with the tide lapping gently at his feet. The sound of the waves should have been soothing, but his mind was turbulent, swirling with the earlier events.

It was supposed to be a simple, peaceful day. The Earthen plane was a world of dangers they weren't prepared for, and today had been a harsh lesson. For a moment, he thought of Thrush, wondering where he was. All of this felt wrong. He'd tried to stay strong for Rue all these weeks, but something was going to need to change soon.

Remington let out a heavy sigh, running a hand through his hair. He turned away from the ocean, ready to head back inside when he heard a faint, distressed mewing. He paused, listening. The sound came again; a sad cry. He followed the sound and it led him back to the beach house. The mewing sound came again, and Remington thought it was from under the porch.

As his curiosity piqued, he knelt down and peered into the darkness. Two bright eyes stared back at him, and a tiny kitten edged forward, its fur matted and dirty. Remington reached out a hand, murmuring softly until the kitten crept close enough for him to scoop it up.

"There, little one," Remington whispered, holding the trembling creature against his chest. He knew about cats, they walked both sides of the Veil. Half in, half out. He straightened, casting one last glance toward the beach.

Inside, Rue was resting on the couch, still pale but smiling weakly at something Chel was saying.

Jed and Shay were preparing dinner in the kitchen and Remington's stomach grumbled at the smell of cooking meat. He missed having access to a fully stocked kitchen all day long. He was hungry here, a lot.

Remington approached Rue, the kitten clutched gently in his hands.

"Look what I found," he said softly, kneeling beside her. Rue's eyes widened, her face lighting up at the sight of the kitten.

"Oh, Remm," she breathed, reaching out to pet the tiny creature. The kitten mewed again, nuzzling into her hand.

Chel's brows rose in surprise. "They have those here too?"

Remington shrugged. "Guess so."

Remington watched as Rue's smile grew, some of the tension easing from her face.

"It's one of us," Rue whispered, rubbing her nose against the kitten's. "It smells like home."

Despite the chaos and danger, this small moment of joy felt like a gift. He knew they had a long road ahead, filled with challenges they couldn't foresee. But for now, this was enough.

"We might not be meant for the Earthen plane," Remington said, watching his sister cuddle the kitten, "but we'll make the best of it while we're here."

Rue nodded in agreement as the kitten licked at her fingers.

Chel patted Remington on the back. "Your father would be proud to see how well you've taken care of your sister today." Chel wished Skeele could have seen it, and that they wouldn't soon learn of their father's fate. Chel had a feeling it wouldn't be long. Call it his Hellion intuition, he could sense something powerful headed their way.

Glass shattered in the kitchen and everyone turned.

Shay was gripping her stomach. She reached toward Jed. "The crossroads are calling," she warned.

"Be careful," Jed said as he leaned forward to kiss her quickly before she was pulled away.

# TWENTY-ONE

Shay and Nero stood at the crossroads. One side of the road was open field, the other pine forest. The air was thick with anticipation, a foreboding sense of doom hanging over them like a shroud. Nero shifted uneasily, his muscles taut with tension. They both knew this wasn't just a routine summons, it had the stench of something far more sinister.

Asmodeus stepped out of the mist. Tall with dark, leathery wings and eyes that glowed like molten gold, his mere gaze made Shay wish Nero would take a step back.

"Hello, Shay," the Demon greeted, his voice a silken purr laced with venom. "So good of you to come when called." He smiled.

Shay squared her shoulders. "What do you want, Demon?"

"I told you we'd meet again." A predatory grin curled Asmodeus's lip. "I've heard rumors," he began, his gaze flickering to the ocean visible in the distance, "of Demons tasting the blood of something that doesn't belong in the ocean. Sweet, innocent blood." He sniffed the air. "It's a scent that's hard to forget. It's tainted the ocean."

Shay's heart skipped a beat. She felt Nero tense beside her, ready to spring into action if needed. "I don't know what you're talking about," Shay said.

Asmodeus tapped his chin. "First it was the auras, now the blood. Blood that has attracted attention. Demons are always hungry for something new, something powerful." He licked his lips.

"Get to the point," Shay growled as Nero snapped his teeth in agitation.

Asmodeus's smile widened. "The point is, I can protect whatever you're hiding. I can ensure your glowing, sweet-blooded creature remains safe from demonic interest... but it comes at a price."

Shay's eyes flashed with anger. "What do you want?"

"The same as last time we met. Alastor's skin trades," Asmodeus said, his eyes gleaming with ambition. "He's beyond simply being overdue and his failure is my opportunity. Give me a deal to take over his operations, and I'll guarantee your safety."

Shay felt a cold chill run down her spine. Making a deal with Asmodeus was a no go. There was already a deal involving Alastor's skin trades.

"The creatures who crossed the Veil will find you. They are *ravenous*." He looked over his shoulder and something growled in the dark shadows of the pine forest.

Nero stomped his front hooves before turning to gaze at Shay. He wanted to burn the Demon to ash.

"Do it," Shay said, gripping Nero's mane.

There was nothing Shay wanted more in this moment

than for Asmodeus to no longer be a threat to them. He knew too much.

Nero whinnied vehemently and reeled back on his hind legs. Asmodeus's golden eyes went wide as the duo in the crossroads changed. Nero doubled in size, his long black tail and mane became stiff as needles and sharp as razorblades. Veins became giant ropes of obsidian, twining and swirling under his skin. Shay changed too. Wild, blue hair whipped in the night wind as she became something wraithlike and powerful.

Asmodeus stepped back, dust coating his leather wing-back shoes.

Nero gnashed his teeth together before heaving forward and throwing flame from his throat.

Asmodeus shouted in guttural Hellspeak, one step ahead of Nero's flame. The Demon danced with fire. Nero took a breath, moved to the edge of the crossroads markings and breathed fire, this time igniting the Demon's pantlegs.

"You will regret this," he warned.

"Do not beckon us again," Shay shouted. "Or you will not enjoy the outcome."

Asmodeus disappeared into the mist without another word.

Nero strutted in the tight summoning circle, before dipping his head and burning the chalk line, releasing them.

"Good, boy," Shay said as she patted Nero's side then leapt down from his back. "Keep us this way," Shay said. "There's someone else we need to talk to."

Shay pulled a black feather from her pocket. She'd carried it for weeks and months, ever since that night the Raven King tucked it there. Shay didn't have Jed's magic, but he'd taught her a few spells she could use. She twirled the feather and whispered words that sounded like the chattering of a dozen birds, then waited.

Shay and Nero paced the roadway. She'd never summoned him before but he needed to know about Asmodeus sniffing around.

The air around them shimmered and crackled with electricity. The moon's silvery glow was suddenly shaded by a creature in the air. Shay focused on the form in the night sky.

Sparrow flew in a tight circle before plunging to the ground, his dark wings folding gracefully as he landed.

"The Crossroads Demons in full regal attention." Sparrow appreciated the duo but kept his distance. "Smells like char." He sniffed the air then glanced at the shadows and fog behind him.

"Nero nearly singed a Demon to death." Shay took in the hollows of Sparrow's face and the way his shoulders curved. "Are you sick?"

"No," Sparrow snapped. "What do you need?"

Shay took a deep breath, steadying herself. "We just had a meeting with a Demon named Asmodeus. He's making threats. He wants Alastor's skin trades." Shay paused. "This is the second time he's summoned us. He offered to take on all of Alastor's debts."

Sparrow's eyes narrowed, his expression darkening. "What else did he say?"

Shay took a few steps closer, nearly as tall as he was in this form. "Asmodeus offered my safety. What is going on in Hell, Sparrow? Have you heard from Meg? I know you'd rather kill her than help her, but this doesn't feel good." She glanced up and down his frame. "And you look like dog shit. I made deals with you. You get my soul in the end. You get Alastor's skin trades. What should we expect next? Am I going to die soon, Raven King?" Panic and rage were flooding Shay. She didn't want to die. She had too much to do and she wanted more time. Plus she had Meg's children to care for. She couldn't take care of them if she were dead.

Sparrow cursed under his breath, pacing a few steps away before turning back to her. "Asmodeus is a dangerous player. He's always been ambitious, but this... this is a new level of manipulation."

Shay's voice was barely above a whisper when she said, "What choice do I have? If he can guarantee my safety, I might have to make the deal." She glared. "And you... you look sick." Shay waved, motioning to his gaunt form. "Tell me what's going on."

"I'm perfectly healthy," Sparrow snapped. "Healthy as a horse."

Nero released a whinny of contempt, not believing any of it.

Sparrow side-eyed the Demon horse. "I am!" he argued. "I just need to eat something."

"You need to release some information to us, now." Shay was growing tired of Sparrow avoiding the truth.

"The Queen of Hell no longer has a throne but she's safe."

"Oh my god." Shay ran hands through her hair and glanced toward Nero. "She's alive?" Where is she?"

Sparrow was shaking his head. "I can't tell you everything."

"Then tell me *something*!" Shay said. "Let me know if

I'm going to stay alive until the end of the week. Demons have been hunting us. We've been on the run. If Asmodeus offers to protect me again, I might take him up on it."

"Don't," Sparrow warned. "Don't you dare." His black wings spread.

"The Veil between Hell and the Earthen plane is thin. I can feel it," Shay said. "The dead will start walking soon. Why haven't the Deacons stepped in yet?"

"I can't tell you everything." Sparrow glanced at Nero. "Just trust me. Please." There was so much he couldn't tell Shay. There was too much resting on Sparrow's shoulders, too many secrets.

Shay studied him for a moment before nodding in agreement. "This war must end."

Sparrow closed his eyes and shook his head. "There are many moving parts which could too easily tumble down to nothing."

"Bring Meg to me," Shay said, clutching her hands. "If she's alive and no longer Queen, bring her to me."

"I'm not making that deal." Sparrow looked away. "There are others who need her."

"Who could need her more than her family?"

Sparrow's head tipped in question. "Watch what you say." He'd wondered where Meg had hidden her child, now he was quite suspicious of Shay's words.

"Me and Jed are part of her family. Just like Noah and Nightingale." Shay clarified.

"And her daughter?"

Shay's lips pressed into a thin line.

"Just as I thought." He glanced toward the shadows of the pine forest. "Plenty could be listening. Babylon wants her to find Lucifer's bones and put an end to Alastor's coup."

"What if he kills her?"

"I won't let that happen," Sparrow's tone was resolute.

"*You* won't?" Shay was watching him closely.

The moonlight cast long shadows behind Shay and Nero as Sparrow launched himself into the air without another word and flew away. Sparrow seemed rushed. Previously when they'd met he lingered almost as if he was bored.

Shay shivered as they returned to their normal forms.

"That was an interesting conversation."

Nero whinnied in agreement.

# Twenty-Two

*Meg*

I stand in the dimly lit room and pack my bag. Moving silently, I gather what little belongings I have. After strapping my blade to my thigh, I reach for the doorhandle. Every sound seems amplified by the stillness of Sparrow's house. I open the bedroom door and tiptoe to the kitchen.

I grab an apple from the countertop and the blood fridge catches my eye. No. I shake my head. No. I don't have time for that.

Standing by the door, I pause for a moment, my hand hovering over the knob. There's no noise. I open it. It seems too easy and makes me wish I'd left before this moment.

I leave before the first hint of dawn touches the horizon. The streets of Sparrow's kingdom are eerily silent, the usual bustle of activity still hours away. I move quickly, my footsteps echoing in the empty corridors, my heart pounding in my chest. Sparrow will be furious when he discovers my absence, but I don't want him by my side for this.

The chilly morning air bites into my skin and I zip my jacket and shiver. The path to Babylon is familiar, yet every shadow seems to hold a threat. I can't afford to be caught. As I walk, my thoughts are a whirlwind of memories and fears. I make my way to the forest path and jog toward the gate that opens to Babylon. The sun is barely up and I'm hoping I can get out of here without being noticed. I flip my hood up and keep it low, avoiding eye contact with the few early risers who glance curiously in my direction. Babylon is a city of secrets and I need to remain one of them.

The fountain finally comes into view, its waters glistening in the faint light of dawn. I approach cautiously, scanning the area for any sign of danger or attack. Nothing. It's a miracle.

I stand at the fountain, ready to jump in and finally see my children after all this time. I feel a shift in the air, a subtle change that makes the hair on the back of my neck stand up.

"Leaving without me?" Sparrow's voice echoes across the fountain with unmistakable firmness.

I look up and see him standing across from me. "I was trying to evade you," I say.

"I think that might be the first truth you've told." His expression is a mixture of concern and disappointment. He adds a cocky smirk after I've been staring too long.

"You wouldn't know," I say, adjusting my bag. My heart races in anticipation.

"Where are we going?" Sparrow asks.

"Peabody Library, Baltimore, Maryland."

Sparrow nods.

I jump.

———

The library looks abandoned, just like it's supposed to. The "Condemned" sign on the door is a nice touch. I walk up the stone steps and reach for the door.

"Let me," Sparrow steps in front of me and tries to open the door but it won't budge.

"It's warded against you," I say, moving to open the door.

"Not against you?" he asks.

"I own the place."

We step inside and close the door. I glance to the floor and step to the edge of the runes. The familiar scent of old books and polished wood is comforting, but an unsettling quiet fills the cavernous space.

"Where are they?" I whisper, glancing around nervously. The library is usually buzzing with warmth, Nero's hoof clops typically echo as he greets whoever is at the door. But he doesn't come. Everything feels eerily still.

Sparrow frowns, his eyes scanning the room. "Looks empty."

Suddenly, a rustling sound comes from behind one of the towering bookshelves. My body tenses, ready for the unknown.

From the shadows emerges an Angel, nearly naked, with disheveled hair and a look of surprise on his face. He clutches a towel around his waist, clearly caught off guard.

"Halt, who goes there?" the Angel exclaims, blinking in astonishment. "Oh, shit." The Angel drops to his knee and bows. "My apologies, Raven King. I never thought you'd ever walk in that door."

"Jasper?" Sparrow sounds surprised and the tone of his voice melts into amused recognition. "We thought you were dead. It appears you've simply run away."

The Angel moves to his feet and shifts awkwardly, his wings fluttering slightly. "Well, I was just, uh, enjoying the amenities of the Earthen plane. You know, hot showers, soft towels, the occasional... leisure activity. Nudity. Women." Jasper walks closer and scrubs his foot across the rune on the floor.

I step away from Sparrow and investigate. "What happened to Jed and Shay?" I ask, trying not to give away too much information. The floors are scratched from Nero's hooves. I notice burned books and a pile of broken shelves. Panic fills me. "What happened here?" I move toward Jasper, gripping my blade. "This looks like an attack."

"Whoa. Whoa." Jasper holds up his hands and glances at Sparrow. "I didn't do anything. I helped them. I killed the Demons that were attacking."

"Demons attacked my..." I hold in my secret, the word *children*.

Jasper is nodding. "There was a whole bunch. They came in the back. There was a break in the wards." He points to the back hallway. "I saw it from outside. I... I fixed it. I didn't hurt any of them. I promise."

"Then where are they?" I ask.

"Please, Raven King, tell her I wouldn't harm anyone."

Jasper is looking terrified and keeps glancing in Sparrow's direction.

"It's true," Sparrow says. "Jasper is harmless. He's a healer in training from a... another kingdom."

"A kingdom that wants me dead?" I ask.

Sparrow clears his throat. "He won't hurt you. Tell us more."

"I was sent to protect someone. A human. I can't say any more about it." Jasper glances to the pile of rubble in the corner. "I've been cleaning up. Keeping the wards, although," he chuckles, "I'm not as good with magic like that half-breed Jed is." Jasper releases a breath, impressed. "Now that guy is something. You should have seen him when the Demons went after that little girl." Jasper looks at his own hands. "That guy has some power."

"What happened to the girl?" I ask, worried that Rue was injured–or worse.

"She's fine. They're all fine. Even that big Hellion. Wasn't expecting to see that guy on the Earthen plane." He motions to his wings then Sparrows. "But the Veil is so thin. Our wings are completely visible these days. I'm sure the dead will start walking again soon."

"Where did they go?" Sparrow asks.

"South. Florida. The blue haired girl, Shay, she had an address." He points to a hallway that leads to an underground garage. "They took one of the vehicles."

"Are you here alone?" Sparrow asks.

"Today I am. Sometimes that Demon horse Nero comes to visit. He likes the organic carrots from the farmer's market."

"Nero visits you?" I ask.

Jasper nods and tightens the towel around his waist.

The Angel just went up a few ranks in my book. Anyone who Nero freely hangs out with must be safe.

I head for the garage.

"Where are you going?" Sparrow asks.

"I'm picking out a vehicle and then I'm heading to Florida."

Sparrow and Jasper follow me to the garage. I flick the light and see that Jed and Shay took the Grand Cherokee. I open a box on the wall that contains all the keys and select the Jeep Commander. It's my favorite out of all of the vehicles I've stashed down here.

"Are we going to discuss this?" Sparrow asks.

"No." I unlock the Jeep. "I don't have much time before Babylon ships me off to Hell to die. I'm going to see my daughter now." I hate that I can't *poof* and travel there in a second.

"Wait, is that..." Jasper sucks in a breath. "Is that Meg? *The* Meg?"

"Not what you expected?" I ask, glancing back to Jasper to catch the surprised look on his face.

"I just thought you'd be," he clears his throat, "taller, maybe. Scary, or something more formidable."

I smile sweetly, innocently.

"Don't test her, bud," Sparrow warns. "She'll rip your throat out faster than you can say hallelujah."

I press the button that opens the garage door. "Are you coming?" I ask Sparrow.

"I'll drive," Sparrow says.

"You won't. You look like shit and you're moving slower than molasses in January." I point to the passenger seat. "Over there." I look at Jasper. "Just so you know, this library is mine. I'll allow you to stay here but fuck with me or my family or friends and I'll gut you in a heartbeat."

Jasper swallows hard.

"Was that necessary?" Sparrow asks.

"Absolutely." I slam the door closed and start the engine. I click my seatbelt before asking, "You're going to get in this enclosed space with me? After making me walk to Babylon?"

———

THE GPS in this old Jeep is pretty much worthless. I head for the highway, taking a turn onto Holliday street, then Baltimore street until I see the signs for Interstate 395 South. I drive too fast, take sharp turns that make Sparrow curse.

We drive the interstate through winding Appalachian mountains. As we approach a rest stop, I am reminded of taking a drive similar to this with Sparrow a long time ago. I remember him bending me over a guardrail in the middle of the night as shadows slithered in the forest below. I speed past every rest stop, refusing to let those memories resurface again.

The endless ribbon of asphalt stretches out before us as I drive into the night, the headlights cutting through the darkness. The hum of the engine and the occasional passing car fills the silence. Sparrow sits in the passenger seat, his usual confident demeanor replaced with a pallor I can't ignore.

"You're sick," I say.

Sparrow forces a smile that doesn't reach his eyes. "I'm fine. Just tired."

I frown, gripping the steering wheel a little tighter. "You don't look fine. If you're not feeling well, you need to tell me."

"I'm fine," Sparrow insists, his voice lacking its usual strength. "We should probably find a place to rest, though. You need a break."

"I don't need a break," I say. "Don't make this about me. I'm in tiptop shape."

He glances at me, unbelievably, from the corner of his eye.

"I can keep driving. We're not too far from Florida now."

"We need to stop for a few hours," Sparrow says, pointing to a sign for a nearby hotel.

"We'll be fine." I glance at the clock. We're only a few hours away from Perdido Key.

"You need to rest." He shifts in his seat. "And I need to get out of this confined space." Sparrow shakes his head slowly, wincing as if the movement pained him. "Meg, please. We need to stop. Just for a bit. Trust me."

My heart thrummed against my ribcage as I try to put the pieces together. Whatever was going on with him is slightly familiar. I search my mind, remembering when he was batshit crazy, when curses took his memories, when turning into a Hellion took his memories.

Reluctantly, I pull off the exit and drive toward the Microtel sign. The neon vacancy sign flickers in the night, casting an eerie glow over the parking lot. I pull into an empty space and turn off the engine. The sudden silence is almost deafening.

"Stay here," I say. "I'll get the room." I motion to his wings. "The poor schmuck working here won't know what the fuck is going on if you walk in there with those obnoxious wings hanging out."

Sparrow nods before closing his eyes and leaning back in the seat.

I hurry inside and talk with the woman at the counter. Her nametag says "Cherry" and she smells like an ashtray.

"Lucky for you we have one room left," she says, tapping on an ancient computer.

"One room?" I sigh. "There was no one on the highway."

She takes a puff from her burning cigarette. "Cause everyone is in bed. It's nearly midnight."

"Oh. Okay." I pass her my credit card.

"Need identification."

I dig in my wallet for the I.D. the Deacon gave me after my trial. The card sparkles and as I pass it to the woman, the image changes to a Florida State Driver's license.

"Hear the beaches are nice this time of the year," she says, passing my cards back to me.

"Yeah," I say. "The water is really warm."

"Okay we have room 7B with a queen bed." She passes me a key.

"One bed?" Something sinks in my gut.

"There's a couch. No pullout bed though." She looks away from me. "Enjoy your stay. Checkout is nine thirty."

"Is there free breakfast?"

"No," Cherry replies absently.

"Thanks," I mutter, taking the key and heading back to the Jeep.

Sparrow gets out of the vehicle as I get closer. We walk to the room, Sparrow's steps slower and more labored than usual. Something is up with him. Usually he's full of vigor and malice. Maybe he needs to eat. Too bad for him.

I unlock the door and go inside where I turn on the light and drop my bag in a dinette chair.

"You should lie down," I say.

Sparrow turns. "One bed."

"It's all they had."

He grunts before crossing the room to the couch and sinking down onto the cushions. He closes his eyes and tips his head back against the wall.

I sit on the edge of the bed, watching him with a mixture of worry and frustration. "Sparrow, what's going on with you?"

He sighs. "It's nothing. Just...I'll be fine after some rest."

My stomach growls. I wish I'd brought food.

Glass clinks.

"Here," Sparrow says.

He's holding out two vials of blood. My mouth waters. I cross the room to take one from him.

"Is this spoiled?" I ask. "I don't want to get sick again."

Sparrow opens the vial in his hand and throws it back like a shot. Blood stains his lips.

"If this is rotten, I'll slit your throat," I warn, cracking the top on the vial.

Sparrow rolls his eyes.

I sniff the blood, then taste it with the tip of my tongue.

It tastes good; warm from being in his pocket and like something... familiar. I drink it all then fall back on the bed. So much for not taking blood from strangers. I kick off my boots and try to ignore the warm feeling blooming in my center. It intensifies. Shit. I sit up, gather a thick breath, and drag air into my lungs. Drinking blood with him was a bad idea.

But, I like bad ideas. Hell, bad ideas are my modus operandi.

Sparrow is staring at me, his cheeks flushed and looking a bit fuller now. Just one vial of blood made him look like he slept twelve hours. Interesting.

He shifts his hips, makes a growling noise like wearing pants is absolutely killing him.

"Come here, Meg," he beckons, reaching toward me like I am something delectable.

Hell, my legs move without my brain thinking logically. All I can think about is last night when his mouth was on my neck and his hands were on my body.

Sparrow's pupils are blown wide, like he's high as fuck. I glance in the mirror over his head and notice mine are the same.

"What was in that blood?" I ask. "Crack? Marijuana? Oregano?"

Sparrow is lounging in a whorish manner. I blink and put the image in a spank bank for later.

He reaches up, grabbing my hips, his fingers gripping the beltloops of my jeans. "Just blood," he finally says, pulling me down to straddle his lap.

In an instant we're breathing the same air and his hands are on my neck, twisting in to my hair. His lips are on my jaw, the gentle glide of his tongue trails to my lips. "Kiss me, Meg," he begs. His voice is commanding yet gentle. "Don't push me away like before."

I do it because I'm too stupid to live. But the moment my lips press against Sparrow's, I don't regret it. I don't regret my tongue gliding against his, or the way my hips grind against the bulge in his pants. And then he's pushing me to stand and pulling my pants down my legs before dragging me onto his lap again. Large hands rub over my thighs and settle on my hips. I fall into him, kissing and grinding and enjoying the way his hands slide over my skin. Every breath is somehow sweeter, and I can't get enough of the feel of him, the smell of him, the taste. I've only waited forever to have him like this again. His hands slip into my underwear and I lean back, tugging my shirt off.

He's watching me, a lazy smile on his face, eyes dark. This is a cocky Sparrow. I've never seen him like this before. I smile back and let the ache in my center take over. I am being sucked into the vortex that is Sparrow. It feels familiar. Strong. It feels like... my stomach clenches as I realize it feels exactly like *bloodlust*.

My hand flies to his throat, gripping just below his jaw.

He smiles darkly.

"What the fuck did you do to me?" I ask, part of me knowing already and I feel stupid for not connecting all the pieces before this moment.

"I did what I had to do." He stares at me, unafraid, lifting his chin so I can get a better grip on his neck.

I squeeze, feel the pulse of his carotid against my fingertips.

"Do it if you want. How many times do I have to die

for you, Meg? How many times before we can finally be happy?" Sparrow asks.

"I never asked you to die for me." I squeeze tighter, but grind against him like I can't control my body. I can't. I'm barely in control. "I could ask you the same question. How many times do I have to die? How many times do you have to break me?"

"I never wanted to do it," Sparrow says, hands rubbing my bare thighs. "I would do it again." The weight of his words hangs in the air, charged with an electric tension neither of us can ignore.

I squeeze my hand tighter around his neck until he closes his eyes. "You would kill me again. I knew it," I say. Something breaks in my chest. This was a bad idea. I should have run from him the first chance I got. I should have climbed out the window or hit him over the head with a shovel or... I should have done something different because now I'm trapped and I'm going to have to explain this mess to my friends and my children.

Suddenly I am in the air and being flipped onto my back. Sparrow is leaning over me, red lines across his neck from the grip I had on him.

"I meant the blood bond," he says. Sparrow's eyes are dark and intense. "I would do it again, a hundred times. I will always want you, Meg. We can't escape each other. We can't escape *this*. Soon we will go back to Hell and we'll need to be top of our game. It's about time you realized the blood bond took. At least now I can stop dripping my blood into a bag or a vial for you to drink from, and we can feed the old fashioned way. I've been hungry. Starving actually."

That's why he's looked like shit for days. He needs to feed from me with the blood bond. I swallow hard. If I feed from him I'll be feeling like a million bucks.

"When?" I demand.

"When I found you with your wings cut off. You were dying." A sadness slips into his voice. "You'd been poisoned and attacked. There was no healing from that without a bond."

I wrap my legs around his waist, moaning when he grinds his hips against mine.

"I know this is a lot to take in," he says, his voice a low, soothing murmur. "But I promise, you're safe with me. It won't be like before. You've suffered too much." His lips press to the scar over my heart. "I can never say sorry enough for what we've been through."

My heart races, a mix of apprehension and an undeniable pull toward him. We've always been connected, a magnetic force has always drawn us despite the chaos surrounding us.

His arms cage my head in place.

"I... I don't know what to say." My voice is barely above a whisper. "This changes everything."

Sparrow's fingers brush my forehead, sending a shiver down my spine. "It doesn't have to," he says, his touch igniting a fire within me. "It only makes us stronger. We will be invincible together. Everyone knows it. That's why they tried to keep us apart for so long."

I close my eyes and take in a deep breath, feeling the warmth of his skin against mine. The world fades away and it is just the two of us in a cocoon of shared history and unspoken desire. I look into his Ireland grass green eyes and find a depth of emotion I haven't seen before. It's all too real. Far too real and it feels like a dream to have him again like this but there's strings attached. A million strings.

"I'm scared," I admit, my chin trembling. "I've waited so long for this. For you. You broke my heart. Left me in pieces. I can't heal from that in a heartbeat. There's a reason why I don't trust a soul. That's baggage. I'll never trust you again."

Sparrow's gaze softens, a tender smile playing on his lips. He cups my face, thumbs gently caressing my cheeks. "I'll fix it. I'll glue it back together like you glued feathers to my wings in that church in Hell so long ago." He searches my eyes. "Please, Meg. Forgive me." He shakes his head as his eyes turn glassy. "I can't take you back to Hell and lose you again. We do this together. We do this strong."

My throat feels thick when I swallow. "And after, then you'll try to kill me again? How do I trust you? I can't survive you again, Sparrow. There will be nothing left of me."

He kisses me quickly. "No. The omens are done, they are fulfilled. We did everything. I did everything they asked."

"How can you be so sure?"

His hand moves behind my neck. "It's the only way. I'll kneel to you every day. I'll do whatever I can to win back your trust." He licks my neck. "Just say yes. Please."

It's the way he says *please* that melts my apprehension and replaces it with a fierce longing. I wrap my arms around his neck, pulling him closer into a deep kiss. "Yes," I whisper because I don't believe any of it.

Sparrow's hands roam over my ribs, his touch igniting

every nerve ending. He breaks the kiss just long enough to whisper against my lips, "Meg, I need you."

"I'm yours," the words tumble out of my mouth breathlessly. My fingers tangle in his hair.

Our bodies entwine in a dance of need and desire. Sparrow's kisses trail down my neck and I cannot control the soft gasps as he tips my head to the side, exposing my neck.

"Do it," I say. "Drink."

"Not yet. Not like this."

Disappointment stabs me in the gut as he moves away and stands. Cool air rushes my heated skin. I prop myself up on my elbows and watch as Sparrow kicks off his boots, then tears his shirt over his head. He tugs his jeans off next. Naked Sparrow is a sight for sore eyes. I don't think I'll ever get tired of seeing him like this in all his glory.

He reaches forward, fingers looping in the edge of my underwear. He tugs them off then advances. His mouth is on my knee, my thigh, the vee between my legs.

My back arches, my head presses into the mattress as his tongue works my body into a tight coil. Soon I'm the one begging please and scratching at his shoulders until he kisses his way up my body, across my belly, his hot mouth stopping at my breast.

"Oh, god, Sparrow." The words come out of my mouth as a wanton whisper.

He rolls us and suddenly he's on his back, black wings spread across the bed, and I'm straddling his hips. Large hands grip my waist. He lines up our bodies and presses inside. It's too much, having him again. I can't control my body as the bloodlust takes over. My mouth falls to his shoulder and I bite. I savor the sweet taste of his blood on my tongue as he fills me.

He rises, sitting up as I ride him.

"Do it," I beg. "Please." His blood stains my lips.

He's holding back, his body tense, a string ready to be plucked. He knows we are both about to lose all control like never before. I feel his mouth on my shoulder, his tongue gliding up my neck, the sharp ecstasy of his bite.

We tumble away to bliss, to carnage, entwined and writhing as one. With blood on our tongues and a promise in our souls, we become one again like never before.

In that hotel room, with the night stretching out before us, we find solace and passion in each other's arms. The bloodlust has taken over. Sparrow will go to Hell with me and for the first time in my life I know in the center of my being that we will triumph together or we will die together.

# Twenty-Three

"I saw Meg sneaking out this morning," Noah said as he poured a cup of coffee and stared out the window like a forty year old dad checking out the neighbor's grass.

"She's going to the Earthen plane," Nightingale said. "Sparrow told me. He's going with her."

"She was alone when I saw her crossing the yard." He sets a pan on the stove and starts cooking for Thrush; eggs and sausage and leftover biscuits. "She probably tried to leave him behind."

"I can't say I blame her," Nightingale said as she crossed the room to sit at the breakfast nook.

"What do you think he's hiding?" Noah asked.

"I have to do some digging. He hasn't exactly trusted me with any secrets after I chose Hell over my family's kingdom."

There was shuffling in the hallway as Thrush readied for the day. He made an appearance a few moments later, grumbling about them being too loud.

"Good morning," Noah said as he grabbed a plate from

the shelf and tipped the contents of the pan onto it. "You want coffee?" Noah asked Thrush as he sat.

Thrush nodded as he picked up a fork and began eating. He'd woken up with a sense of unease gnawing at him and spent the early hours of the morning staring at the ceiling, listening to the distant sounds of Sparrow's kingdom coming to life.

As he ate, he finally broke his silence. "I don't want to be here any longer," Thrush declared, his voice firm. "I can't stay here anymore."

Noah and Nightingale made eye contact, exchanging worried glances.

Thrush swallowed his bite of food. "I want to go to wherever Remington and Rue are."

Noah spoke first, his tone resolute. "Thrush, this is the safest place for you. Alastor's forces are everywhere in Hell."

Nightingale nodded in agreement, her eyes filled with concern. "We only want to protect you, Thrush. This kingdom has the strongest defenses. Leaving would be too dangerous."

"You died here, mother. How safe could it be?" Thrush's frustration bubbled to the surface. "I can't stand it here," he argued. "I need to do something, be somewhere I can make a difference. Our lives have been ruined by Alastor and we are just sitting here. Meg is going to go back to Hell to face Alastor and she's going to die."

"How do you know that?" Noah asked.

"I just know." Thrush stood up and left for Legion training. "I need to do something, be somewhere I can make a difference."

Without waiting for their response, Thrush went out

the door. His mind was a whirlwind of thoughts, his focus scattered. As the day progressed, his distraction became evident. He narrowly avoided several accidents during battle drills, his mind consumed elsewhere.

The Legion Angels around him began to notice. They made crude jokes. "What's got you so distracted, Thrush. Is it a girl?" one of them taunted, making horns with his fingers, and throwing kisses in Thrush's direction.

Thrush ignored them, pushing through the training with gritted teeth. By the end of the day, he was exhausted and bruised, his mind no clearer than it had been that morning. He missed training with the Hellions and learning spells with Jed. He missed Remington and Rue.

At dinner, his parents tried to engage him in conversation. Noah mentioned exploring more of the Seven Kingdoms and possibly visiting Gabriel's kingdom for a few weeks. Thrush didn't participate more than a few nods of his head.

After eating, Thrush excused himself and went to bed. He lay there, waiting for the cabin to fall silent. Sometimes his parents went to the Astral plane at night, but never for long.

Thrush quietly slipped out of bed. He moved through the darkened halls stealthily, his heart pounding in his chest.

He didn't see his parents anywhere. Returning to his room, he grabbed his bag and began packing. He found a change of clothes, weapons that he'd brought from Hell, and the books he'd dried out. That was all he had. His room was quite barren even though they'd been living in the cabin for weeks. This wasn't home to him, or his parents, no matter how much they tried to deny it. None of them had settled in. He'd heard his father mention Meg had left that morning and she could only be going one place, to see Rue and Remington.

Thrush made up his mind.

He tucked pillows under his blanket to make it look like he was sleeping in bed. Then he opened the window and climbed out.

Cool air brushed past his face. While the days had been hot, the night was cool and windy. There was a stone wall that bordered the Raven King's lands, so he stuck to the shadows of the tree line and made his way to the trail that led to Babylon.

He paused a few times, hearing voices in the distance. Angels from the Legion barracks were wandering.

"Sneaking out to see your demon girlfriend?" one of the Angels had seen him.

Thrush went still, gripping the knife in his pocket. "Yeah," he said with a light chuckle.

The Angel laughed, then muttered something about filthy blood and walked away. The guy didn't care that Thrush was sneaking out. It was just another reason to get the heck out of this place. This was not home. Not a soul cared about him here.

He jogged down the trail that led to the gate of Baby-lon. His heart was thrumming against his ribcage as he stepped across the threshold to his family's lands. He itched his head, thinking about the family curse of turning crazed if he didn't do his time as a Hellion. Thrush didn't care. He was going to find his friends.

He made his way to Babylon, navigating thought the park-like sidewalks with ease. The sounds of water splashing echoed through the night. The fountain was straight ahead.

Thrush took a notebook from his pocket. He'd started collecting spells just like Jed. While Thrush didn't necessarily have magic like Jed did, he had a tiny spark inherited from somewhere along his bloodline that allowed him to cast some spells. He flipped through his notebook and found the spell he was looking for.

Thrush stepped up on to the fountain, his boots hanging off the edge. He took a breath of the clean Heaven air and held a hand over the water while he chanted to spell which would reveal where Meg had gone earlier this morning.

The water bubbled and steamed for a moment before turning smooth as glass. Meg's image appeared, and he saw her exit onto the Earthen plane.

Thrush closed the notebook and tucked it in his bag. Guilt flooded his chest. He'd never been without his parents, and he knew they'd be severely disappointed in him. But Meg had saved his life before, when he was an infant, and Thrush would always owe a life debt to her, even though she'd dismissed it as nothing. He couldn't stand by any longer.

His mother would find him in dreams. Thrush doubted he'd get far without them showing up. They'd just have to understand that he was ready to grow up.

Thrush took one last gulp of air before stepping into the portal.

He paused as the water stirred. And then, a hand appeared. Thrush waited as someone came through. There was nowhere to hide so he stepped down and waited, thinking of an excuse if whomever came through the portal asked who he was, or, worse, tried to attack.

Thrush tightened the strap of his pack and pulled the knife from his pocket. He took a defensive stance, just like the Hellions had taught him and waited.

"Holy crap," he said, joy and concern flooding his chest. Securing his weapon and reaching forward, Thrush grabbed the hand and pulled them to the edge.

# TWENTY-FOUR

*MEG*

THE JEEP ROLLS to a stop outside the beach house on Parasol Place. Down the crushed shell road, white sand stretches out before us like a promise of peace. I take a deep breath, trying to steady my racing heart. The drive from the hotel was tense, filled with unspoken words and furtive glances. Now, as we sit in the Jeep, the weight of my secret feels heavier than ever.

"Well, here we are," Sparrow says, his voice casual, but I can hear underlying tension. "You ready?"

I nod, avoiding his gaze. "Yeah, just... give me a minute, okay?"

Sparrow frowns. "What's going on, Meg? You've been acting strange since we left."

"I want you to wait outside," I say. "I don't want you to come in with me."

Sparrow's eyes search mine, looking for answers I'm not

willing to give. He rubs his face. "Okay. I'll wait here. But not for long."

"Got it," I murmur, opening the car door and stepping out. The sea breeze hits me, bringing with it a sense of urgency. I have to get inside before Sparrow can see what I've been hiding.

The problem is, I don't get a chance to knock on the door and surprise my children in secret. They must have seen me from the window because they come bounding out.

"Mother!" Rue exclaims. "I was so worried." She throws her arms around me and I grip her tight. She's taller and thinner and I regret missing time watching her grow. But I don't regret hiding her away and keeping her safe. I notice her limp.

"What happened?" I ask.

"We were swimming in the ocean and I was bit by a shark." Rue twists her leg and shows me fading marks on the bottom of her leg.

Remington leaps off the porch and runs toward me. "You're finally back!" he throws his arms around me and Rue.

"Where's father?" Rue asks. "Is he coming too?"

There is a strange noise behind me, something that sounds like the garbled sound of a man being strangled. Something thuds on the ground.

"Who is that?" Jed shouts as he runs across the crushed-shell driveway. "No! No!" Bright light flashes from his fingertips. "How could you bring *him*?"

Shay and Chel run out of the house next, rushing

toward us, ready to fight, ready to defend just like they've always promised they would.

"Wait," I shout, holding out my hand to stop Jed's attack. "Just... *wait*."

I turn and find Sparrow on his knees, his face pale, eyes watery. Shock and awe don't look so good on him.

I told him that I didn't want him to come and this is why. Rue looks suspiciously like me and... Nightingale. I spent plenty of time lying about genetics but there was no hiding Remington's heritage, because he was the spitting image of his father.

Sparrow.

Now I was going to have to explain the biggest lie in all the realms. The secret I've kept for nearly fifteen years. The secret Teari kept. The secret Shay and Jed have kept. The Hellions too. These are Sparrow's children. Not Skeele's.

I never told Sparrow. And I still don't want him to know. That's too late now. I can't lie my way out of this mess.

"Where is father?" Remington asks. "Did you defeat Alastor? Are we going home?"

I shake my head. "I must tell you both something." I take their hands. "Your father, Skeele, he died a hero. I did not defeat Alastor and I must go back and face him again. I wanted to come see you both just in case it's my last time."

# Twenty-Five

*Then*

TEARI WAS RIGHT. It was eighteen months. Eighteen months of apologies, forgiveness, and getting my shit straight.

When the birth finally came, there was no bloodbath like in the books she showed me. There was no gore or torn apart vaginas or vacant eyes. The birth was quiet. The parts of me that hurt during and after, Teari healed almost instantly. Skeele held me and fed me and brushed my hair out of my eyes when Teari set the naked baby on my chest.

"She has dark hair, like you," Skeele said.

I touched his horns and asked, "Not these?"

"No." He shook his head as the baby let out a blat. "She's mouthy like you too. Looks like she has your temper."

Now here's the part I didn't tell you. The part I hid

because no one could know. The part that everyone close to me swore to secrecy.

Skeele is staring at the baby. He's in love, I think. Real love, true love. The kind of love only a father can have for his daughter. But the first wave of unease hits me when I see her eyes. I glance to Skeele. His eyes are black as night.

My stomach lurches then cramps start again.

"Teari..." I call.

"I'm here. It's alright." She moves closer and touches my leg. "It's the afterbirth. You have to deliver it."

"Okay." I nod and get ready. My abdomen cramps. "It feels like contractions again."

"Just push it out. Easy," Teari soothes. "This is all very normal."

I'm nodding even though something doesn't feel right.

"Push when you're ready," Teari says.

I'm nodding until the cramping is too much, then I'm pushing. I feel her hands on me.

"Oh Lord," Teari whispers.

"What is it?" She said this would be easier but it feels like I'm giving birth all over again. Sweat breaks out across my forehead. I find myself squeezing the baby on my chest.

Skeele is holding my hand. "Give her to me," he says, prying my fingers off her little shoulder. "Let go of her, Meg. Here, hold my other hand."

I glance at him, panic in my eyes. He's holding the baby girl with one hand, and my white-knuckled grip has his other hand. I don't know what to do or what to think. My blood feels like it's equal parts fire and ice.

"What's happening?" I ask, unable to hide the panic in

my voice. "Am I going to die? Is this death? Is something tearing me apart from the inside?"

Teari's scrambling to collect supplies. "Everything is fine," she murmurs. "Just fine." She lays a clean towel over my stomach then opens a fresh supply kit. "You're going to have to give us a big push now, Meg. Bigger than before."

"Why?" It comes out as a whimper.

"Because there's another baby. I don't know how I missed this." She curses under her breath.

"Another fucking baby? No. No." I'm shaking my head frantically. "You're wrong. It can't be."

"It's okay," Skeele is saying from my side.

The baby he's holding starts to cry.

I start to cry.

"Teari, why?" I ask. "Why is there another?"

A contraction cramps my belly and I push as hard as I can.

"Good. Take a rest." Teari touches my abdomen, feeling for the next contraction. "The head is right there. This should be quick."

I'm nodding and sobbing and squeezing Skeele's hand as tight as I can.

The contraction starts.

"Now," Teari says.

I push, grinding my teeth together, pushing through the pain.

"Okay, take a rest. The baby will be out on the next push." Teari rubs her hands together then holds them over my abdomen using her magic to ease my pain.

"Why is there another baby?" I ask again, looking

between Teari and Skeele. I didn't plan for this. I thought my belly was so big because of all the pizza and waffles I ate.

"Now," Teari says.

A contraction comes and I push. Things happen, the burning pain, the sounds of Teari's medical supplies. "Okay, relax. On this next contraction this one will be out."

My body pushes the baby out and my head hits the bed. "Please tell me there's no more," I mutter, holding my hands over my face.

Teari moves closer and sets a wet, calm baby on my chest.

"Congratulations, it's a boy," Teari says.

"Where did he come from?" I ask.

Teari chuckles. "You. He came from you."

I peer down at the baby boy. "Where did you come from? I wasn't expecting you." I laugh, exhausted and delirious.

The baby looks up at the sound of my voice and I bite my lips together. Something's not right.

I grip Skeele's hand.

"Teari, we have to talk," I say. "This baby is not part Hellion."

Teari moves closer and takes a better look. "Their faces can be swollen."

"Don't bullshit me," I say.

Teari pauses before nodding, knowingly. Something strange has happened. These babies are not part Hellion. Whatever books Teari was reading about my pregnancy were wrong. Completely wrong.

"It's fine," Skeele says, moving to set the baby girl next to her brother. He kisses me and looks into my eyes. "I know," he says. "I can see it in her." He motions to the little girl. "But they are yours and mine. Do you hear me? They are a gift. The halls of Hell have never seen such fortune. I am proud to call them mine." He kisses me again and nothing but pride washes over his face.

"I wish–" I start to say.

"Shh." Skeele shushes me. "I don't." He shakes his head before settling a large hand over the baby's backs. "I could wish for nothing more." He wraps his arm over us. He turns to Teari. "The second one never came. No one can know. It will be the best kept secret in Hell. He must remain hidden at all costs. Only the few closest to us will know. We'll make up a story. He is the spitting image of his father. He will be in much danger."

Teari is nodding, then shakes her head from side to side. "No one can know. He is a shadow heir." She swallows hard and her color changes to pale as a sheet. "No one."

The Hellions made a bassinet out of dark stained wood. And they quickly work through the night making a second one, sworn to secrecy. They will die with the knowledge of the shadow heir.

———

"How?" I ask Teari when she visits the next week. "I need answers."

She bites her lip. "I read every book in Babylon. But all I can think is that Sparrow is something different. Without his grace, I can't explain how or why. It can only be a miracle."

"That's not going to work for me."

Teari throws her hands in the air. "I don't have answers. I've never seen anything like this before. It's not like I can go to the Archangels and ask them if they've ever seen this before."

"I hadn't been with Sparrow for months," I remind her.

"You could have been pregnant the whole time." Teari shakes her head in disbelief. "The eggs could have been fertilized and embedded themselves late. Heck, maybe his sperm lives for a really long time."

I make a sound of disgust. "I can't believe any of this."

"All I know is that those babies are royalty, Meg." She sits next to me. "You are the Queen of Hell. He is a King of Heaven."

"Their father nearly killed me." Emotion swells in my chest. "He will try to kill me again. And them..." I glance at the sleeping babies. They do look angelic with their cherub cheeks and red lips. "How do I tell them their father is–"

"Skeele," Teari says. "Their father is Skeele." She nods matter-of-factly.

"Yes," I say. "I will tell them their father is Skeele."

# Twenty-Six

Something broke within Sparrow that moment he saw Meg's children bound out of the little beach house to greet their mother. He'd never met the girl before, didn't care to know anything about the daughter of a Hellion. He'd always wondered why Gabriel kept his distance from his grandchild. But Sparrow's gaze flicked between the two teenagers. *Two.* They were either very close in age or... twins. The girl reminded Sparrow of his sister; long hair, green eyes, childlike joy–but she had a streak of Meg's darkness. That was easy to see in the tip of her chin and the dark glint in her eyes. But the boy... the boy was like going back in time and looking in the mirror.

Sparrow sat back on his heels and took a deep breath before standing.

"I won't hurt anyone," he assured Jed and Shay and Chel, who'd surrounded him with weapons drawn and magic flickering. "I promise."

Sparrow stepped back and blinked, waiting for Meg to explain. When she simply stared at him with a blank expression, he grabbed her arm and motioned toward the nearby beach. "We'll need a moment to talk," he told them before dragging her away.

Each crunch of the crushed seashell road under his boot was like another piece of his nearly cold, dead heart solidifying to ice. Meg didn't fight as he dragged her. It was unlike her.

Sparrow finally stopped and released Meg. He rubbed his face.

"Is there something you want to tell me?" he asked Meg.

She pressed her lips into a straight line and glanced toward the Gulf of Mexico.

"You can't run from this." He bent down so they were eye level. "Tell me."

Then it burst from her like a tornado, like a demon on fire. She had held so much in for so many years. Meg could not contain it any longer. "Tell you what?" she sneered. "You want me to confess to you that I've been hiding those children since the day they were born? You want me to tell you they aren't yours? What do you want me to tell you?" Meg's hands went to her hips. "Do you want me to tell you how I had to keep them a secret so *you* wouldn't kill them on the day they were born?"

"I wouldn't–"

"Be careful what you say, *Raven King*. Don't tell me you wouldn't have hurt them because you hurt me. You nearly killed me. And you threatened to come back and finish the job many times." Meg pointed a finger in his face. "You don't get to make me feel guilty for keeping them away from you, for keeping them *alive*."

Sparrow's hand closed around Meg's fingers that were pointing at him accusingly. He pulled her knuckles to his mouth and kissed them softly, eyes closed. No hate. The omen had always been true. So much of it. He cursed the Archangels for what they'd made him do. But, if he hadn't done it, if he hadn't set the slate clean, there would be no safe place for them anywhere on any plane.

"You'll all come back to my kingdom," Sparrow said. He demanded.

"No." Meg was shaking her head. "No, they will not step foot in the Seven Kingdoms of Heaven. They are not safe there."

"Did you see them, Meg?" Sparrow's hands moved to her shoulders. "Jed marked them with runes. Something happened. They are not safe here. They will have the protection of my Legion and Gabriel's. His lands border mine. There is no safer place for them."

Lightning struck the nearby beach and Meg was instantly reminded of the day she was struck not far from this very spot. There was a strange energy in the air that made her uneasy.

Sparrow looked up at the sky and the dark clouds headed toward them.

"There's too many of us here. Too many where we don't belong." He turned her toward the beach house. "We must leave the Earthen plane."

---

MEG AND SPARROW walked across the beach of white

sand, then the crushed shell road. Everyone was watching them warily from the porch.

When Sparrow finally stood before them, his presence commanding and urgent, he said, "We must leave the Earthen plane. I will give you sanctuary in my kingdom within the Seven Kingdoms of Heaven."

Shay exchanged a worried glance with Jed. "Leave the Earthen plane? You can't be serious," she said.

Chel, leaning against the porch post, furrowed his brow. "What's happened now?"

Lightning struck on the beach.

"There are too many of us in one place. This is God's land. The balance is off." Sparrow motioned to Meg's lightning scars.

Jed shook his head, pacing. "This doesn't sound right. I can't go there." He pointed to his chest. "Those Angels have been trying to kill me my entire life. I'm a dead man there."

"They will leave you alone," Sparrow promised. "I said I will give you sanctuary. All of you."

Rue and Remington sat on the edge of the porch. Sparrow avoided their glances, unable to fully deal with the reality of the children.

"I am a Hellion. When has a Hellion ever been allowed in Heaven?" Chel asked.

"It will be allowed," Sparrow promised. "You'll be protected by powerful wards. No Archangels will cross into my territory. No Demons either."

Shay bit her lip, her gaze shifting to the sky. "What about Nero? I can't leave him here alone."

Sparrow shrugged. "What's one more?"

Meg, who had been silent, stepped forward, her eyes resolute. "Sparrow's right," she said firmly. "We can't stay here. It's too dangerous, more dangerous once I return to Hell. The Veil is too thin. My children are coming with me."

Lighting struck, closer this time.

"Please come with us," Meg begged her friends.

"Why should we trust him?" Jed asked, pointing to Sparrow.

"He's changed," Meg said. "He's going back to Hell with me."

Sparrow nodded, "You have my word. Noah, Nightingale, and Thrush are already there."

Remington's face lit up at the mentioning of his closest friend. "I'll get my things," he said before standing and rushing inside.

Shay glanced at Jed and then Chel, who both nodded in agreement. "If we're all in agreement, then we'll go," Shay said, her voice steady. "I'll need to find Nero."

"Where's the closest portal?" Jed asked.

"You're living right next to the largest portal on the Earthen plane." Sparrow pointed to the Gulf of Mexico. "Right there. Sounds like you've been swimming in it. No wonder the girl was bit by something. It was probably a Demon from another realm."

"Wonderful," Shay said with a sigh.

Lighting struck, closer to the beach house this time.

"We need to go," Sparrow urged.

Shay found Nero wandering the beach, and he galloped closer after hearing her frantic calls. She filled him in on the plan as though he spoke perfect English.

Remington had his bag packed and was standing by the door in half the time it took everyone else to pack.

Rue tucked the kitten into the half empty pocket of her bag, leaving plenty of room for air. The kitten was small and didn't take up much space. Rue held the bag across her front as though it contained the most precious cargo.

Jed and Shay gathered their belongings and closed up the beach house. Jed set wards of protection and set spells to the food so it wouldn't spoil.

Meg and Sparrow moved the vehicles into the yard and waited.

Chel didn't have much besides the few items of clothing that Jed had found for him. He carried the items in a plastic grocery bag.

Dark clouds had collected over the beach, promising a thunderstorm. Rain was falling in a gray sheet over the Gulf, headed their way.

"Now would be a good time to go," Sparrow warned.

The group walked to the beach and into the water, Demon horse included.

# Twenty-Seven

The portal shimmered in the morning din, the surface of the water rippling with energy. One by one figures emerged from the fountain. Remington came through first, someone grabbing his hand and pulling him to the surface. As his vision cleared, he recognized Thrush.

"Remm!" Thrush shouted, his voice cracking with emotion.

Remington's head snapped up at the sound of his name. He looked up from the hand gripping his wrist and his eyes landed on Thrush. A grin spread across his face, and he pulled Thrush in, closing the distance between them in a heartbeat.

"Thrush!" Remington cried, gripping his friend in a tight embrace. "I can't believe you're here!"

Sparrow watched the reunion with a guarded expression, his eyes flickering to Meg as she exited the fountain. He needed to get everyone back to his lands quickly, before too many of the Angels saw them and began spreading rumors. He needed to converse with Gabriel before the

Babylon court began asking questions. He also judged his nephew's presence at the fountain. No one knew that they were coming back, which could only leave one explanation for why Thrush was there. The little shit was about to run away. Sparrow's gut twisted as he glanced at the two children whom he shared blood with. The threat of their family curse reared its ugly head times three. The stakes were much higher now. He'd need to speak with Thrush and Remington.

Shay and Jed exchanged glances, the weight of their journey momentarily lifted by the joy of seeing Thrush and Remington together again. Chel clapped Thrush on the back, offering a smile and a joke.

Nero shook, spraying water drops over everyone before he strode out of the fountain and began inspecting the new realm.

"We need to move," Sparrow said, breaking the moment of the children's excitement over being together again. "Heaven or not, we're not entirely safe here."

Meg muttered something about fucking stupid Angels as she helped Rue out of the fountain and motioned for the boys to follow.

Thrush's earlier plan to run away dissolved.

---

SPARROW HURRIED the group to his kingdom and locked the gates behind them. He instantly regretted not building his home bigger when he considered where everyone would stay. He hadn't built a castle like most. There were the outlying cabins but he worried about the children being further away.

———

SPARROW STOOD outside the gates of Gabriel's lands and waited. The Archangel was walking closer and motioned for the gate to open.

"Sparrow," he said, glancing over the Raven King's shoulder. "I heard a story about you coming through the Babylon portal with a gaggle of people." He held the gate open as Sparrow entered and slammed it closed.

Sparrow motioned to a clearing further away from the kingdom's border where they could speak privately.

"I took Meg to visit her daughter as we promised," Sparrow said, slipping his hands into his pockets and rocking back on his heels.

"Good," Gabriel nodded.

"There's just one thing." Sparrow leaned forward, eyes like daggers. "Have you set eyes on your granddaughter lately? She's about fourteen now."

"I've stayed away, at Meg's request." The old Archangel's eyes glistened. "I wish to know her and see her." He rubbed his white beard. "I wanted things to be different. I lost so much time with Meg."

"I brought her back," Sparrow said. "And others. There was plenty of lightning threatening us on the Earthen plane. Too many beings that didn't belong."

Gabriel made a questioning gesture, wanting more information.

"I need your allegiance now more than ever," Sparrow said.

"Of course," Gabriel agreed.

Sparrow knew Meg's father was the most open-minded of all the Archangels and sought not only peace but an end to the broken families of the Seven Kingdoms of Heaven.

Sparrow considered telling him exactly who he was hiding in his kingdom but decided against it. "Meg and I must return to Hell shortly, as soon as she reveals where Lucifer's bones are."

"I take it she is still your prisoner?" Gabriel asked. "And the others you've brought back. Are they prisoners as well?"

"She remains a prisoner," Sparrow said. "The others are... complicated."

"Once Lucifer is resurrected, a larger battle will be on our doorstep," Gabriel warned.

Sparrow nodded. "You should ensure my gates stay locked while I'm gone."

"Keep it under shadow," Gabriel said.

Sparrow thought about the bunkers in the mountain. There was space for plenty, but he didn't think mixing Angels and creatures of Hell was a good idea.

"I might need a few rooms," Sparrow said.

Gabriel was shaking his head. "I can't."

"Your kingdom is not under threat. There is no war at current." Sparrow thought for a moment. "What are you hiding?"

Gabriel's brows rose in non-answer before he motioned to the gate and for Sparrow to leave.

# TWENTY-EIGHT

Nero explored the Raven King's sliver of Heaven. He couldn't find any rips in the Veil that separated Heaven from Hell and the Earthen plane. He considered how he would travel between realms. He kept searching; there had to be a weakness in Heaven's Veil.

Something didn't sit right in Nero's blood. He definitely didn't belong here. There was a constant buzzing behind his neck that reminded him. But, he did enjoy the sweet grass that grew along the Legion training grounds and the fresh water of the nearby pond. Everything tasted different here, better. The blasted sun was hot on his back and he sought shade as he watched the Legion of Angels train. It was a stark contrast between the Hellions training with their leathery wings and heavy thuds on the dirt. The Angels fought with an air of nimbleness and every so often, a white feather would drift across the sky. Nero thought of the Angel at Peabody Library, Jasper. He'd said his name but didn't give much more information.

Nero wandered, searching for entertainment. He

thought it odd that there were no other horses here. Then he wondered what a heavenly horse would look like.

There was a noise at the forest fringe. Nero followed it, hoping to find a slit in the Veil for easy movement between realms.

The forest became denser, the shadows of ancient trees creating a maze of dark and light. The only sounds were the crunching of leaves under hoof and the occasional rustle of a hidden creature. Nero's dark eyes scanned the landscape, searching for any sign of movement. He sniffed the air hoping for the scent of the Earthen plane or the whiff of brimstone. He considered going back to the Earthen plane to find the wild horses again, although, they hadn't been very welcoming when he'd approached them last time.

Nero searched for hours. The ambling had driven him into the heart of Sparrow's kingdom. The forest was quieter here, almost unnervingly so, as if the trees themselves were holding their breath. Nero's steps slowed, his instincts telling him something was nearby. He let out a soft whinny, hoping for a response, but the silence persisted, thick and unyielding.

He waited longer. Probably too long. Just as he was about to move on, a flash of white caught his eye through the dense foliage. Nero froze, his breath catching in his throat as he saw it again–a gleam of pure white against the dark greens and browns of the forest. He stepped closer, careful not to make a sound, his heart pounding with antic- ipation.

As he pushed aside a low-hanging branch, the forest opened up into a small clearing bathed in dappled sunlight. And there, in the center of the clearing, stood a horse unlike any he had ever seen. Its coat was the color of freshly fallen snow, gleaming in the soft light as if it had been crafted from the very essence of purity. Its mane and tail flowed like liquid silver, and its eyes—large and dark—were filled with a calm intelligence that took Nero's breath away.

Nero stepped into the clearing, a soft whinny releasing from his throat. His movements were slow and deliberate. He'd come across wild horses on the Earthen plane and they were always skittish of him. The white horse lifted its head, meeting Nero's gaze with a quiet curiosity. There was no fear in its eyes, only a sense of understanding, as if it had been waiting for him all along.

He could feel magic in the air, a subtle hum that seemed to resonate from the white horse itself. It was a creature of some other kind, it was something more—something ancient and powerful hid beneath its gentle exterior.

For a long moment, the two horses stood there, silently acknowledging each other. Nero felt a connection, a bond that went beyond words or gestures. It was as if they had known each other for a lifetime, though they had only just met.

A sense of peace washed over Nero, easing the tension that had gripped him since he began his search for a split in Heaven's Veil.

Angels were flying overhead, blocking out the fading sun. Suddenly, the white horse huffed, then turned and took off at a gallop.

Nero whinnied and went after the white horse. He followed the flick of snowy tail weaving between trees and overgrown shrubs. The ground shifted so they were running uphill, the ground became rocky, the trees sparser, and the white horse was further and further away. Nero couldn't believe it. He was fast, the fastest creature on any plane. But this white horse was faster. Soon Nero cold no longer see any spec of white in the distance and he slowed as the forest fringe opened to a wall of rock. He paced the base of the mountain, saw no hooves, smelled no other horse.

# Twenty-Nine



*Meg*

IT FEELS good having everyone together again. It's like we're on vacation in a hot, sunny hellhole where none of us belong–AKA the Seven Kingdoms of Heaven. Thrush wasn't so wrong in his opinions about this place.

"Tell me about the boy," Sparrow says, closing the door and locking it.

"He is a shadow heir. Very few know of his existence." I take a few steps away from the looming form of the Raven King.

"Tell me why," he demands.

I let truth spill from my mouth like a river. "Every day I looked at my son and saw you and I loved him. I love him. Can you imagine staring into the face of your enemy every moment of your life and tucking away the hate and the fear? My son didn't make me feel that way, but you did. I had to raise him with love." I was shaking now, years of anger and sorrow that I'd tucked away rising to the surface along with the distress of keeping the secret, of others finally finding out. I search Sparrow's gaze but I can't gain much. "But now you know. I'm guessing all bets are off. His life will be more at risk than ever." Emotion swells behind my eyes. "At least he has a chance to survive now that he's older."

"And the girl?" Sparrow says.

"She is a daughter," I point out. "No one will care much about her. She will be wed or bred." I hate saying the words. That sentence inflames my ears worse than all the times I've said fuck. "Or maybe I won't let that happen. Maybe I'll hide her away so none of you can hurt her. I'll take her somewhere safe so she can live a normal life."

"You're not going anywhere," Sparrow says.

"I have my freedom."

"No, you don't." Sparrow grabs my arm.

I wretch it away. "I delivered the feather of truth. I'm free. Babylon told me so."

"Where are you going to go, Meg?" Sparrow asks. "You can't go to Hell. You can't go to the Earthen plane for long." His fingers trace over the black scar down my arm. "God will cast you out again."

"I'll be good. Promise."

"You're never good. You're bad to the bone. Always have been. Always will be." His eyes drift from my lips to my neck. "You can't go back to Gabriel's kingdom; I know for a fact he does not want to deal with your bullshit."

"He's my father."

"That doesn't mean he must give you a place to live." His fingers drift to my wrist. "And we have the Bloodbond.

You can't go far. You're mine. Your freedom is very limited."

"Bastard," I say between gritted teeth.

"We must deliver Lucifer's bones." Sparrow pushes away from the wall. "Then we will discuss what happens next. But you are not free. You will stay here. As long as you starve yourself." He's too close to me. "Feed. Now. I will not have you going into battle at half a tank."

"I hate you," I say, knowing it's a part lie. I doled out my heart to him at that shitty hotel in the mountains.

"I know. I love it," he mutters with a smirk.

"You hate me."

"That's not true."

"The children?" Who could not hate me for keeping such a secret?

He's silent for nearly a full minute. "Just disappointed. I wish it could have been different."

"Are you going to tie me up then?" I ask. "Chain me in a dungeon somewhere?"

Sparrow smirks. "Why would I do that?"

"That's what kings do to prisoners."

"No, little Night Owl, you need this..." he closes his eyes and rubs his hand over his heart, "sickness inside you like your body needs a spine. You may survive without it, but how deformed and misshaped you'd become. I don't need chains when we have blood that ties us."

I scowl at the nickname once given to me by another. "I loved you and you devastated me," I remind him.

He licks his lips, shifts his wings. The sound of his belt buckle echoes in the sparse room. "You are mine. You will always be mine until one of us dies, again." He shreds his shirt and tosses the scraps away. "Call it what you want. Prisoner. Lover. Bonded. Until you come to terms with it, you will be a prisoner. That's not what I want for you, but you will not leave me again. I can't bear it." He reaches for me, pulls me forward, and our chests slam together. His hands slide into my hair and tip my head as warm lips press against mine.

It's all true. Every word of it. I don't trust him but these words are truer than rain.

"Don't forget," he whispers against my lips. "That I am your prisoner as well. And we have been chained when together and when without each other. It's been written in the stars, our souls perfectly formed puzzle pieces. No one else will do for either of us. We will be invincible together," he reminds me. "Where are the bones, Meg?"

I take a deep breath. "On route 37, there's an old barn with bones in the rafters."

Sparrow groans. "Of all places."

Then I feel his teeth on my neck and I tip my head away offering more.

# THIRTY

<br>

SPARROW WAS COOKING. HE'D NEVER ATTEMPTED to cook for others in his entire life. So far, he'd burned the pancakes, the eggs had a strange texture, and the only thing that seemed edible was the bacon, and that's only because bacon is good half raw or thoroughly burned. He considered making more bacon.

The first person to enter the kitchen was the girl. Rue.

She stopped in her tracks and watched him, warily.

"Are you hungry?" Sparrow asked.

"Kings don't cook." Her hand settled on her pocket protectively.

"Maybe I'm different," Sparrow said as he took a stack of plates out of the cupboard and set them next to the trays of food.

Rue moved closer, apprehensive. "My mother told me not to take food from strangers."

"Smart. I'd suggest the same."

"So I shouldn't eat this?" Rue pointed to the bacon.

"I'm not a stranger."

"Yes you are."

Sparrow pressed his lips together. Meg hadn't told her the truth, and as far as the girl knew her father had recently died in battle defending Meg against Alastor.

A soft mewling sound came from the girl's pocket.

"What is that?" Sparrow asked.

"My kitten." Rue held a hand over her pocket.

"Get it out of here."

"And bring it where? It's mine. I won't get rid of it. I love it." The small kitten meowed from Rue's pocket and its head popped out.

"I hate cats," Sparrow sneered.

"How could you hate a creature so innocent and sweet?" Rue's green eyes were judging him and her forehead wrinkled in scowl. She picked up a plate and began serving herself. "This better not make me sick," she warned.

Sparrow recognized that she sounded exactly like her mother.

Meg walked through the threshold next. She was wearing jeans and a wide-neck T-shirt and looked exactly like the first moment he saw her in Noah's grandmother's basement. So human without her wings. She glanced at Sparrow and proceeded to ignore his existence. Sparrow knew she had a lot to recover from and trust wasn't something he'd earn quickly, even if she needed his blood to survive. She defied him by piling her plate full of food and never looking at him once. Judging from Meg's vibe, she wasn't going to have much to do with him today. Sparrow knew this meant she'd deny him and herself blood until they were both so strained they would come together with the force of a tornado, spitting threats at each other and shredding clothes.

The boys wandered in with Shay and Jed.

"I'm starving," Thrush said.

Remington and Thrush joked and nudged each other as they filled their plates.

The serving plates were empty, all the food gone, and Sparrow decided to have bagged blood and ward off the hunger.

Sparrow opened the black fridge and poured the blood in a coffee mug. He microwaved it warm and went to the dining area and found a seat next to Remington. He wished he'd had time to speak to the boy, but Remington and Thrush had been inseparable. The boy didn't notice Sparrow sat next to him.

It was different having all the noise in the house. Sparrow glanced around the table, a warmth spreading through his chest. He looked down at his mug and thought about his and Nightingale's upbringing, the family curses, the threats from Babylon. He tapped his finger and pulled his wings tighter against his back and thought about the Christmases that were celebrated on the Earthen plane, and holidays with a full table of family and good food. He'd have a lot of work to do if that was his future. He wondered how they could hold this all together after returning to Hell to hand over Lucifer's bones. They'd have a war, instantly. Sparrow blinked and committed the scene before him to memory knowing that it might be his last and only one.

Something warm rubbed against his ankle. Sparrow looked down and saw the furry kitten that had been in Rue's pocket. He reached down and picked it up.

"Maybe you're not so bad." Sparrow muttered as he set the kitten on his lap. It licked his hand then put it paws on the edge of the table and stood up, sniffing his mug.

Sparrow glanced up and found everyone staring at him. He glanced to his left. Remington was staring. Green eyes, familiar eyes. Sparrow searched the boy's face and dark hair.

"You two look alike," Rue said.

"Me and the cat?" Sparrow asked, trying his best to deflect.

"No. You and my brother." She was pointing a piece of bacon at them.

A fork clanged against the floor.

Someone cleared their throat.

# OMENS OF DARKNESS (VEIL OF SHADOWS 13) [UNEDITED]



## CHAPTER 1

*Meg*

I sit in Sparrow's living room, tracing the intricate designs carved into the armrest of an old wooden chair. This place is too quiet, almost eerie in its stillness. I wish Rue and Remington were here with me but they went to explore. I sigh, letting the tension drain from my shoulders. It reappears as soon as I remember I need to sit Rue and Remington down and discuss Sparrow with them. Maybe after that, I won't feel so tightly wound. This secret I've kept too long has been eroding me from the inside. I just want to be free of it now that the children are old enough to manage the truth. Although, I'm still worried about Remington's safety.

The front door creeks open, the sound startling me out of my thoughts. A woman steps into the room.

She is tall, her hair a cascade of golden waves that catch the light and make her look like the ethereal creature she is. She's wearing a white dress that clings to her curves, downy white wings stretch as she takes another step. A smile plays on her lips as her eyes scan the room, until the land on me.

"Oh," she says, her smile faltering. "I didn't realize Sparrow had company."

My jaw tightens. Something about her presence ignites a fire within me, a possessiveness I've been trying my darndest to ignore.

"Who are you?" I ask, my voice sharp. I don't bother to hide my annoyance.

She blinks, taken aback by the venom in my tone, but she recovers quickly, giving me a smile too sweet to be genuine.

"I'm Lyra. Sparrow and I go way back."

Lyra. Sounds like a strumpet.

"Well, Lyra," I say, standing up and crossing the room until I'm just a few feet from her. Damn she's tall. "Sparrow doesn't need anyone from 'way back' at the moment."

She raises an eyebrow, her smile turning sly. "Really? Because last I checked, he and I have unfinished business."

The challenge in her voice is clear, and it sends a surge of irritation through me. If this is Sparrow's old girlfriend, good for her, I don't want her seeing my children. I don't want her around me. I want her gone.

"Whatever business you think you had, take it elsewhere," I say, my voice low and threatening. "Sparrow's not here."

She glances over her back and down the hall. "I'll just go check his room."

"Don't," I warn. "Go."

Lyra chuckles, the sound grating my nerves. "Let me tell you something, sweetheart, you're not the first, and you won't be the last." Her eyes narrow. "Wait a minute. Are you..." she takes a few steps back.

I flash a smile.

"You're the biter." Her hands fly to her neck.

I smirk remembering the time I flashed here and ripped Sparrow's *other* blonde girlfriend out of his bed and bit her neck. That was kinda rude of me. But I was searching for revenge at the time. Can't blame a girl for that.

I step closer, my eyes narrowing. "You're right. I do bite." I snap my teeth.

For a moment, we stand there in silence, the air between us crackling with tension. I notice the doubt flicker in her eyes, her bravado faltering. I get the feeling she might have expected someone to be here but didn't anticipate me. Story of my life.

Lyra rolls her eyes as she steps back. "Fine. Whatever. He's all yours. But don't be surprised if he comes looking for me when things get boring."

That's it. I lurch forward and Lyra turns tail and runs out of the house. I chase her to the doorway, my heart pounding in my chest.

Lyra takes to the sky and something sinks in my chest. A phantom ache stretches across my shoulder blades. I'll never fly again. I watch her go. He'd be better off with someone like her, someone whole.

*"Don't forget," he whispers against my lips. "That I am your prisoner as well. And we have been chained when together and when without each other. It's been written in the stars, our souls are perfectly formed puzzle pieces. No one else will do for either of us. We will be invincible together," he reminds me.*

A dark figure with black wings appears, following Lyra off the Raven King's lands. I cross my arms and watch. Maybe I should have bitten her. I lick my lips. If she were royal lineage it would have given be some more time before caving and dragging my sorry ass to Sparrow's room to beg for a meal. My mouth waters at the thought of drinking from him. Then, instantly dries at the thought of him with another female.

I rub my eyes. Heck, I was with Skeele for nearly fifteen years, I'm sure Sparrow was with someone. I glance to the sky. Or many someone's. Can't blame him too much.

When they are out of view I pace the porch. The thought of Sparrow's old girlfriends handing around pisses me off and worries me. I don't want anyone snooping around. I step off the porch and start walking toward Nightingale's cabin in the distance. Jed might have to lay some more wards.

## CHAPTER 2

"Lyra," Sparrow called as he landed, boots hit the ground mid-step. The air around him crackled with dark energy. She'd always been slippery, finding her way into places she didn't belong. But this was different–this was personal. And he wasn't going to let it slide.

The woman was trying to avoid him now, walking with long strides until Sparrow caught up and grabbed her upper arm.

"Stop running," he called out, his voice cold and sharp, slicing through the silence.

Lyra stopped but didn't turn around immediately. When she finally did her face turned pale at the sight of him. "Sparrow," she greeted, her voice light. She glanced at where his hand gripped her arm. He released her. "I knew you were fucked up, but you're keeping that thing in your house." She pointed toward Sparrow's lands. "How could you. The fallen Queen of Hell. It's disgusting."

"I'm not going to answer any of those questions," Sparrow said, eyes narrowing as he stared her down. "How did you get past my gates?"

She smirked, tilting her head. "You know me. I have my ways."

"That's not an answer." Sparrow growled, his patience wearing thin. "You've always been good at slipping through cracks, but you should not have been able to breach my lands. Someone helped you."

Lyra's spine straightened. "Your Legion let me in. I

wasn't aware that I had been banished. I thought we had something." She reached toward him.

Sparrow caught her wrist before manicured fingers could touch him. "Things have changed."

"But she bit–"

"I know. I was there." Sparrow stepped closer to her and squeezed her wrist. "Why did you come?"

"I wanted to see you." She searched his gaze. "I wanted to invite you out. We used to have fun."

Sparrow didn't trust her. There were plenty of female Angels he'd used for their bodies and their blood. He shouldn't have let his time with Lyra linger over the years. It had only created a problem. A promise she's assumed.

"We aren't going out ever again," Sparrow said. "There's nothing between us. It's over. Ended a long time ago."

Lyra batted her eye lashes before glancing up and down his body. "What will the girls think? They'll all be heartbroken. Some of us really thought you'd pick a girl to settle down with." Big eyes glanced in the direction of his kingdom. "It must be lonely in that big house all alone."

"That was never going to happen. You all knew it." He squeezed her arm harder and pulled her closer. "You have an agenda and I'm not going to let you get away with whatever game you're playing."

Lyra met his gaze.

"I have never trusted you." Sparrow's voice was dangerously low. "And I don't believe for a second that you came here just to hook up."

Lyra's expression hardened. "Maybe I was curious.

Maybe I wanted to see what was so special about what you're hiding in there."

"This place," he said, tone icy, "is mine. And it's off limits to you."

"What else are you hiding beyond that gate?" Lyra tried to pull her arm back, but Sparrow had gripped her so tight it was causing bruises.

"None of your concern. Tell whomever you're working with."

"Protective aren't we? What's the matter, Sparrow? Afraid I might tell the wrong people about your little secret? Afraid I might tell someone you have the fallen Queen of Hell hiding out in your kingdom? What other creatures are you keeping there? Babylon will have a field day with this."

Sparrow grabbed Lyra's throat and squeezed. Sharp teeth flashed as he dragged her close. "Now, listen carefully, you're never going to mention Meg being in my home. You're never to mention her name or presence to anyone. And you're never to come here again."

He squeezed her throat tighter until breathing ceased and her eyes turned red. "Nod or die."

Lyra was still.

"This isn't a game. If you value your life, you'll heed my warning. Stay out of my lands. Stay out of my life. And stay the hell away from Meg."

She finally made the slightest nod of her head.

He released the Angel woman and pushed her away. Disgusted.

"Fine," she spat.

And then she was gone, disappearing down the pristine walkway toward Babylon.

Lyra was a problem he'd been able to ignore for years. He'd ruin her if she didn't keep her mouth shut.

# From the Author

Guys, I can't believe there's only one more book left in Meg and Sparrow's story. I've been writing this series for nine years, and it's so hard to let them go. But don't worry—this won't be the end of the *Veil of Shadows* world! Up next is Sparrow's story, set during his time away from Meg. After that, we'll dive into Rue's story, followed by Jasper's (the Angel living rent-free in Peabody Library). I'm also thinking about giving Remington his own story. So don't be sad—there's plenty more to come!

# About the Author

M. R. Pritchard delves into the profound clash between good and evil, the mystical realms of gods and monsters, and the intricate transformations of ordinary people into beings of immense power. Her gripping narratives often unfold within the haunting backdrop of apocalyptic or post-apocalyptic landscapes, offering a unique blend of suspense and wonder.

M. R. Pritchard is a two-time Kindle Scout winning author, her short story "Glitch" has been featured in the 2017 winter edition of THE FIRST LINE literary journal. Her short story "Moon Lord" has been featured in Chronicle Worlds: Half Way Home (Part of the Future Chronicles) and will be time capsuled on the moon on the Lunar Codex in 2024.

Visit her website MRPritchard.com and Subscribe. You'll get subscriber only content, deleted scenes, updates, special previews of new projects, and book deals.

Veil of Shadows Series:

Sparrow Man

Nightingale Girl

Scarecrow

Raven King

Nightjar

Night Owl

Etched in Darkness

Embrace the Night

Shadows of Destiny

Midnight Serenade

Echoes of Treachery

Omens of Darkness


Thread the Bone


<u>Fantasy/Fairy Tale Love Story/Romance:</u>

Muse

Forgotten Princess Duology

Midsummer Night's Dream: A Game of Thrones


<u>Poetry/Short Stories</u>

Consequence of Gravity